ABOUT THE BACHELOR TOWER SERIES

Ruth Cardello's Bachelor Tower is now a world where every apartment is occupied by a hot bachelor. Garry F. Brockton created an all-male haven for ambitious men who want to live like kings and play by their own rules. Casino nights, a fully equipped gym and lap pool, cigar and Scotch bar, and a media room with screens the size of the average movie theater. The list is endless. Men use the connections they make there to launch their careers or stay at top. It's impossible to get into and even harder now that Brockton's niece inherited after his death. She's trying to shake the place up, for now it remains a haven for ambitious men. The best part: the tower attracts women, beautiful women who hang out in the lobby bar and vie for an invite upstairs.

Under new management the place has a bit of a curse:

Lately, even the most die hard of the bachelors have been falling in love...

BONE FROG BACHELOR

Bone Frog Bachelor Series

SHARON HAMILTON

SHARON HAMILTON'S BOOK LIST

SEAL BROTHERHOOD BOOKS

SEAL BROTHERHOOD SERIES

Accidental SEAL Book 1

Fallen SEAL Legacy Book 2

SEAL Under Covers Book 3

SEAL The Deal Book 4

Cruisin' For A SEAL Book 5

SEAL My Destiny Book 6

SEAL of My Heart Book 7

Fredo's Dream Book 8

SEAL My Love Book 9

SEAL Encounter Prequel to Book 1

SEAL Endeavor Prequel to Book 2

Ultimate SEAL Collection Vol. 1 Books 1-4 /2 Prequels

Ultimate SEAL Collection Vol. 2 Books 5-7

BAD BOYS OF SEAL TEAM 3 SERIES

SEAL's Promise Book 1

SEAL My Home Book 2

SEAL's Code Book 3

Big Bad Boys Bundle Books 1-3

BAND OF BACHELORS SERIES

Lucas Book 1

Alex Book 2

Jake Book 3

Jake 2 Book 4

Big Band of Bachelors Bundle

BONE FROG BROTHERHOOD SERIES

New Year's SEAL Dream Book 1

SEALed At The Altar Book 2

SEALed Forever Book 3

SEAL's Rescue Book 4

SEALed Protection Book 5

SUNSET SEALS SERIES

SEALed at Sunset

Second Chance SEAL

Treasure Island SEAL

Escape to Sunset

The House at Sunset Beach

SILVER SEALS SERIES

SEAL Love's Legacy

SLEEPER SEALS SERIES

Bachelor SEAL

BONE FROG BACHELOR SERIES

Bone Frog Bachelor

STAND ALONE BOOKS & SERIES

SEAL's Goal: The Beautiful Game

Nashville SEAL: Jameson

True Blue SEALS Zak

Paradise: In Search of Love

Love Me Tender, Love You Hard

NOVELLAS

SEAL You In My Dreams Magnolias and Moonshine

PARANORMALS

GOLDEN VAMPIRES OF TUSCANY SERIES

Honeymoon Bite Book 1

Mortal Bite Book 2

Christmas Bite Book 3

Midnight Bite Book 4

THE GUARDIANS

Heavenly Lover Book 1

Underworld Lover Book 2

Underworld Queen Book 3

Redemption Book 4

FALL FROM GRACE SERIES

Gideon: Heavenly Fall

NOVELLAS

SEAL Of Time Trident Legacy

All of Sharon's books are available on Audible, narrated by the talented J.D. Hart.

ABOUT THE BOOK

I have done it all. I have built three global security companies, including foreign subsidiaries which include an airline company and a shipping conglomerate, partnered with some of the biggest industry titans in the realm of international trade. But my love is in protecting and securing the safety of those I care about.

And I've done this, as it turns out, at the expense of my own security and fortune. I've cared for everyone else's assets, and left mine wide open to plunder.

Well, that was then. This is now. This is me fighting back. I'm going to screw that b**** of a former wife, who, while she was screwing me in my own bed, was slutting with other men. I was naive, but now, fully awakened, I will have my revenge.

And it will be sweet!

AUTHOR'S NOTE

I always dedicate my SEAL Brotherhood books to the brave men and women who defend our shores and keep us safe. Without their sacrifice, and that of their families—because a warrior's fight always includes his or her family—I wouldn't have the freedom and opportunity to make a living writing these stories. They sometimes pay the ultimate price so we can debate, argue, go have coffee with friends, raise our children and see them have children of their own.

One of my favorite tributes to warriors resides on many memorials, including one I saw honoring the fallen of WWII on an island in the Pacific:

"When you go home
Tell them of us, and say
For your tomorrow,
We gave our today."

These are my stories created out of my own imagination. Anything that is inaccurately portrayed is either my mistake, or done intentionally to disguise something I might have overheard over a beer or in the corner of one of the hangouts along the Coronado Strand.

I support two main charities. Navy SEAL/UDT Museum operates in Ft. Pierce, Florida. Please learn about this wonderful museum, all run by active and former SEALs and their friends and families, and who rely on public support, not that of the U.S. Government.
www.navysealmuseum.org

I also support Wounded Warriors, who tirelessly bring together the warrior as well as the family members who are just learning to deal with their soldier's condition and have nowhere to turn. It is a long path to becoming well, but I've seen first-hand what this organization does for its warriors and the families who love them. Please give what your heart tells you is right. If you cannot give, volunteer at one of the many service centers all over the United States. Get involved. Do something meaningful for someone who gave so much of themselves, to families who have paid the price for your freedom. You'll find a family there unlike any other on the planet.
www.woundedwarriorproject.org

CHAPTER 1

Marco

I HAVE DONE it all. I built three global security companies, plus foreign subsidiaries including an airline company and a shipping conglomerate. I used my skills and training as a former Navy SEAL and partnered with some of the biggest industry titans in the realm of international trade. But my love has always been in protecting and securing the safety of my country and those I care about.

And I did this, as it turns out, at the expense of my own security and fortune. I cared for everyone else's assets and left mine wide open to plunder.

Well, that was then. Now I'm fighting back. I plan to screw that bitch of a former wife who, while she was screwing me in my own bed, was slutting with other men. I was naive, but now, fully awakened, I will have my revenge.

It's a very simple two-step process: One: Get even.

Two: Create massive success by re-capturing the wealth I lost playing the marriage game. Payback and wealth creation are the best forms of revenge a man can conjure up. Maybe it wasn't the road to happiness, but it's the road I'm taking, with my team of specialized agents. My revenge would be sweet, and the screwing her over wouldn't have any bedroom on the horizon.

Happiness was an illusion. I believed being happy was running hard and screwing harder next to a woman I thought was a racehorse, like myself. She ran a lean takeover operation of my assets. Maybe she would have upped it to the optimum level, since we had no children. She would have been my sole beneficiary. While I wasn't looking, the person I thought I was closest to dug in deep through opportunity and, yeah, because I'm a good guy at heart.

No more. Fuck Mr. Good Guy. I'll be taking no prisoners. I'm a vacuum cleaner in a phonebooth full of million-dollar bills. And yes, they do exist. The Treasury Department printed some for me so I could frame one to hang in my office.

Tony Abruzzo told me about The Bachelor Towers (lots of sound effects there...or at least there were every time he spoke those words). He said it was mostly inhabited by younger men of my ilk. Up-and-comers and monied trust fund babies who could be my sons, if I'd been a bad boy in high school and knocked someone up.

At first, I wasn't interested. I was still seething from the betrayal Rebecca had played against me, taking half my wealth and costing me most of the other half defending what I had left. The anger was fresh with me. And since I never gave up, I knew it would never go away until it was satisfied. Those fires quenched.

I remembered that conversation well—when he "sold" me on the idea just like he'd sold me Bentleys over the years.

"Marco, one thing's for sure, with the average bachelor age being around thirty-five, there won't be many women over that age. Ripe, beautiful. Looking for love and money. And I'll bet many of them are tired of boys—or boys trying to behave like real men. You've got the experience they crave. Been a Navy SEAL and have the scars to prove it. You came from nothing and carved your way out with years doing hard time on the battlefields and used it to your advantage. You're smart. You're lean and primed for some old-fashioned good times you so richly deserve."

"You're forgetting one thing, I'm focused on revenge," I told him that day.

"Even better. They love men who are driven to obsession."

"Why would that be?"

"Because a man who can't fight can't fuck. You remember that quote from Patton?"

"Yeah, we used to say it every night in Coronado after we got our leave."

"Women love to be the object of desire by a man who knows better. Not a man who is beginning to get the lay of the land. They want an experienced lover who will ride them wet and leave them panting for more. You're the original Italian Stallion, Marco. You're the guy they've been looking for their whole lives."

I must have looked skeptical, but I was seriously chewing on the idea.

"Here's an added bonus," Tony said as he sipped his purple martini that looked like it could be a Dr. Death cocktail. "You don't even have to tell them to flaunt it in front of your ex. Women love to do that shit all the time. It's human nature to them. It's the, "'see what a prize you threw away?'" stuff. Wars were fought over this, Marco. You know I'm right."

He had several valid points, and then I investigated.

So here I was, walking into the marble foyer of the Bachelor Towers in Boston. It wasn't much to relocate from New York City proper, and I was done with that whole life anyway. Boston had plays and musicals, opera, art galleries, museums and parks. And before I decided, I spent a day just walking around the city, finding its people were real, gritty, and not snobby like New Yorkers could be. It had great restaurants, lots of movers and shakers there. I would still maintain my apartment in D.C. so I could slip in and out without detection and with the security and anonymity I required since a lot of my business was generated there. Rebecca didn't know about the safe house in Coronado and the lot in Florida, if the shit really hit the fan.

And it almost got that bad.

Everything that was important to me was in the small black leather duffel bag with the Bone Frog logo on it in my left hand. My right hand held a half dozen hangars of suits I couldn't bear to part with. These had been specially made for me in Hong Kong and South Korea, sewn of the finest wool and linen blends, the seaming thread so lightweight it almost floated. Everything else I left with the brownstone in New York. I even left her my jewelry and my wedding ring. I didn't want any taint of it permeating my new life as a bachelor.

Since the reception desk was empty, I looked for the person whose job it was to greet the residents of the Bachelor Towers, the person who I would probably get fired. I crossed the lobby to the neat bar sparsely packed with couples and three-somes, speaking in hushed tones. A piano player tinkled the ivories in the background. The bartender, Oliver, I'd been told had been stolen from the Waldorf. Hired for his discretion, he knew the tastes of just about any living legend, down to the number of orange peel slices, shavings or sizes of the ice cubes. I needed a drink badly.

"Sir? What do you require?"

I liked his attitude right away. His green eyes and slight brogue were charming. He'd taken this job to come home, I deduced.

"Something muddy, smokey, with an orange aftertaste. Not too sweet. Give me my next favorite signature drink, please, Oliver, if I may call you that?"

He surveyed the clothing I was carrying. "You may indeed." Placing a coaster on the countertop he snapped his fingers. A young, handsome Filipino bellman relieved me of my load, moving in the corner of the bar, in the shadows like a clothes tree, awaiting further instructions. Again, very impressive.

"And what may I have the pleasure of calling you, sir?"

"I'm one of your new tenants, Marco Gambini." I hesitated to mention the vacant front desk, knowing it might be career-ending, but I decided to go with truth. "And your front desk is missing an attendant."

"Yes, Brent is attending to a little escort out the back of the building. It's where we deposit the detritus, and it's unfortunate you happened to come along during that moment. I'm sure he'll be back shortly.

And I apologize. This is on the house, Sir."

He pointed to a deep purple/cobalt cocktail floating with some heady orange cream liquor, the red pitchfork plastic stir had skewered a bright red cherry. I liked the visual of the screwed cherry, though I didn't like things too sweet. I sipped. Hint of fizz. Orange and roses aftertaste. Pure sex. I was hooked.

I held the squat etched glass up to him, "Perfect. What do you call it?"

"Midnight in Manhattan, sir."

"I like it even better."

I loosened my tie and unbuttoned my shirt. I felt comfortable studying the room. A young, very lean, blonde girl came up to me, sort of like the house pussycat. With practiced grace and subtle fragrance in a form-fitting dress that revealed how perfect her body was, she joined me at the bar.

I usually like to talk last. This time, I was going to tell her I wasn't interested, but she beat me to the punch.

"So you are the legendary Marco Gambini, the billionaire SEAL?" She interrupted my possible answer to give her command, "Ollie, another one of those for me, with two cherries, please, and don't let him pay for it."

That's when she turned to me and I did like what I saw.

"You're timing is poor, sweetheart. I'm no longer a

billionaire."

"Oh, I think not. I don't judge men by their performance but by their potential." She glanced me up and down like a man does to a beautiful woman. "I'd like to be your first date, sort of a "'welcome to the family'" kind of fuck, if you'd do me the honor."

She got me laughing right away, and that was a good sign. I liked women forward, assured, and beautiful. She was nearly half my age, and that worked too, in all sorts of ways.

Brently Morrison, the front desk manager, burst into the bar, his hands wringing, breathless. "I'm so sorry, Mr. Gambini. We had a difficult situation, and I was pulled—"

"Brent, I think we're good," interrupted Oliver. "If you can show Lujan here to Mr. Gambini's room, he'll hang these things up for our new resident." He turned to me. "Is that to your liking, sir?"

As I leaned back into the bar, the blonde moved close enough that I could feel how her body breathed, something I always loved about a woman. "Just one drink, and then I'd like to get settled. It's been a long day."

With another couple snaps of his fingers, Ollie sent Lujan, my suits, and duffel with Mr. Morrison. I still had the Glock tucked into the back of my pants since I never could get the feel of wearing a holster for the animal. I turned and caught her forcing a stabbed cherry between her red lips, biting and chewing it while gazing at me with steely light blue eyes.

I figured Oliver would have warned me if she was a working girl. I had always thought sleeping with women other than my wife to be a stupid hazard many a man regretted later. Especially without a blood test or background check.

But I was getting reckless in my old age. In my rage. Or maybe I was mistrusting my new-found freedom when it came to women. I'd always been tightly bound in my commitments, still fingering the groove left behind from fifteen years of wearing a wedding ring. Moving in here would be a doorway to my new bachelor lifestyle and I liked to stake out the terrain, notice the little things that could result in a failed mission to guard the safety of my men. I turned around just to make sure Rebecca wasn't there watching me take the morsel dangled in front of me—someone I knew I'd thoroughly enjoy.

But the coast was clear. I was ready to launch.

Permission to engage, you bastard. Make it so! I told myself.

She was lovely to look at and I allowed my heart to melt just a little at the edges like a dark piece of chocolate on a warm plate.

"I know the name of this building. I know the name

of this drink. I *don't* know *your* name," I whispered, leaning into her.

She didn't answer right away but devoured the other cherry in front of me, tearing at it with her bright white teeth, daring me to grab her and kiss her sweet lips, which of course I wasn't going to do in public.

But I thought about it.

In my fantasy, she was naked, displaying her perfect ass as she lay a path of rose petals in front of me while I walked barefoot, crunching them with each step.

She gave the perfect answer. "You don't need that, Marco. I know what you need."

Well, all right then.

CHAPTER 2

Marco

BRENT BROUGHT ME my key card. "We will have your touchpad completed tomorrow, if that suits you, Mr. Gambini," he said, handing the platinum key to me.

"Thank you."

"I have a bit of orientation to give you, when you are ready, so just ring me up." He handed me his card. "That's my cell, and I answer it twenty-four hours a day. It's a special line for our residents here."

"Thanks again," I said as I slipped the card in my breast pocket. She was still rimming her drink with her forefinger. Ollie was waiting on a pair of young bucks halfway down the bar.

"We've taken the liberty to stock your apartment with some staples. We understand you prefer Coppola, so we've had it flown in. You'll find a case of it waiting for you. We have some cheeses and specialty fruits in season from our farmer's market. Next to the basket is an order sheet for anything we left off. We know you like Black Rifle coffee and drink it with half and half, so that's all provided for you, along with a grinder and French press."

I continued to be impressed, although it violated one of my cardinal rules.

"I'm going to have some boxes delivered in the next day or two, mostly clothes, but a few other items I've purchased, including a big screen for office work. I don't like anything delivered to my quarters without me being present."

"Of course, Sir, for security."

"So this will be the last time this occurs, is that clear?"

"Yes, sir. We have storage upstairs outside your quarters. Would it be acceptable to leave things there, or would you like to approve them first?"

"I'd like to see them before they're placed anywhere near my front door."

"Very good, sir. Will there be anything else?"

"No, I think you've done a fine job, Brent." We shook hands. As he began to walk away, I called out, "What sort of problem was it that involved the rear entrance?"

Brent blushed. "Of the female kind, sir. It happens." He shrugged. "It was a request of the resident.

Nothing we couldn't handle, although we don't make a habit of it." He finished his sentence without looking at the blonde.

Good on you.

Oliver approached and asked if we wanted a second, just in case I'd changed my mind. "Not for me, although it was delicious," she smiled, pushing her empty glass forward. Her red fingernails matched her lips perfectly.

"I'm good. I'm going to be addicted to Midnight in Manhattans," I said.

"In the morning, we'll make you my orange juice wake-up elixir best had with fresh biscuits and strong black coffee, Breakfast in Boston. You'll like that one too, Mr. Gambini."

I took her arm without asking. As we crossed the marble foyer to the elevators, it occurred to me I hadn't eaten in several hours. The drink had been strong and I liked how it kicked in. But my mind was far from food.

She was easy on my arm, adjusting herself as we stood in the elevator just so her left thigh lightly pressed against mine and my forearm grazed her breast. It had been a long time since I'd dated, and even though my libido heightened, which I liked, I didn't want her to see me nervous, which I didn't like.

On Floor Twelve, we exited, walking into a mini landing room that doubled as a small sitting area.

Several locked doors were lined up around the room, probably my personal storage areas Brent had mentioned.

I tapped the key card against the glass square on the door marked 1212, heard the click, and entered my new apartment.

The drapes had been opened, and a stunning view of the Boston city lights displayed before me like a tray full of jewels. I'd seen pictures of the scenery in the daylight, panoramas of the harbor and surrounding area, but not at night. This was every bit as beautiful as the glistening columns in Manhattan I called home for fifteen years.

A large bouquet of flowers was on the coffee table in the living room. Off to the side and open to the huge room, was a stunning kitchen with black granite countertops, appointed with black-tinted stainless steel appliances, just as I'd ordered. I had decided I'd learn to cook, and I supposed it wouldn't be something most the men in this building did, which didn't bother me one bit.

She was behind me, telling me she was ready whenever I was. And I was.

My arms encircled her waist as I pulled her into my body. I arched her backward, feeling the heat of her quivering mound. Her soft face looked up to me, her arms up over my shoulders, her lips slightly parted, ready.

I dove in with a kiss I wanted to remember. The first of many. I knew by the way she sighed and moaned that she'd be good for me, to help me forget—just for the evening—that I was a mean motherfucker bent on revenge.

I took her hard, but was careful not to hurt her. We went over the threshold together. The two of us. In a barrel. Over the Niagara Falls.

In her arms I found solace. Her legs spread wide and her sweet moist sex restored me to the man I'd always been. I was grateful for the anonymity, the lack of competition in the fucking I'd told myself I loved with Rebecca. She was no comparison to Rebecca. She matched me in every way, sometimes leading me gently into rooms I'd not been inside during my long monogamous marriage. I was thrilled to be bridled by her beauty, her strength. It was long and sweet and I was fully satisfied, but not totally sated.

I think she was surprised how quickly I'd undressed her outer shell, peeled the layers of whatever had begun to build in her young life. She probably wasn't prepared to have any feelings for me whatsoever. But I could tell she did. As I came inside her the first of several times, savoring her shattering body beneath me, she turned her head, and I, always the gentleman, pretended not to see her soft tears. It was a surprise to me, too, that I liked seeing those tears.

My last memory of the night, before I dozed off to sleep, was the lovely lady tucking herself into my chest. My arms naturally cradled her body as if she needed protection. But she didn't beg. She just accepted the strength of my arms and my chest, with her chin tucked down, her hands up to her lips in fetal position.

She didn't ask for more than I gave and I didn't give more than she asked for.

SHE WAS GONE from my bed when morning sun shone through the sliding glass door in the master bedroom. I'd always thought it better to send a woman away with something more than she walked into my life with. I used to think that way before Rebecca. And she was the only exception to this rule.

As I lay there, still smelling her sweet scent, I thought about what was fair. Rebecca had made the mistake of taking first advantage. I'd now start yanking it all back, and then some. I wanted her to rue the day she first met me.

I rose, throwing on the new silk robe left for me draped over a burgundy leather occasional chair. Cinching the waist, I padded out to the living room and open kitchen, looking for her. Her perfume still lingered in the air.

"Hello?" I asked.

But there was no answer.

"I would call your name if—" But I knew she'd gone.

It was a first-class move and made her easy to be desired, a mystery to be pursued.

Picking up the house phone, I ordered the biscuits Oliver had recommended, some fresh jam on the side, and a bowl of strawberries.

"You want the Breakfast in Boston as well?" he asked me.

"Well, of course."

"And how was your evening, sir?"

"Spectacular. Do you know how to reach her?"

"She left her phone number with me in case you asked."

Another nice touch.

"Who is she?"

"I do not know. Have not seen her before, Mr. Gambini. But she came looking for you, that I know for sure. Brently has her personal information. Her address and place of employment were verified. I'll ask Mr. Morrison to send this up with your biscuits. Would that be acceptable?"

"Of course, I'd like that. Any guesses?"

"Well, your residency isn't exactly a secret in Boston. Neither is your divorce."

"But, this isn't Manhattan, so I thought—"

"The old money lives here, Mr. Gambini. But I'm sure you've been told this before. We make it a habit of knowing everything about our residents and their guests. Guests, especially the ladies, have to be vetted first to hang out at the bar, unless accompanied by a gentleman of the house."

After grinding my fresh Blackbeard's Delight coffee and pouring the boiling water into my new French Press, my doorbell rang. My order of fluffy biscuits—accompanied with three small bowls of apricot, blackberry, and strawberry jam, along with whipped butter and strawberries and cream arrived. A plain brown manilla envelope was sealed on the side, with my name on it.

Her name was Shannon. And she lived in Florida, of all places. She was fifteen years younger than I was. She had pursued a modeling career but was working at a Tampa television station, TMBC, as a stringer and part-time weather person.

I touched her picture, as if my forefinger could somehow pick up some of the missing pieces of her life. But the connection, if there had been any, was not there. I would have to find out because I certainly intended to call.

Beneath the envelope was a folded Boston Herald newspaper. My picture was front and center.

D.C. Power Boss Retreats to Boston. Tail be-

tween his Legs.

It was the sort of headline Rebecca would have written. I picked up the silver tray and threw it against the wall. Biscuits, jam, and the lovingly prepared Breakfast In Boston drink flew in all directions.

I ran in search of my Glock.

This. Meant. War.

CHAPTER 3

Marco

I WAS IN the shower when the cleaning service let themselves in and began removing the mess my anger had created. I did give permission not to be the one to let them inside, as long as Brent did it. I felt a twinge of embarrassment, like a piece of my dirty laundry had been exposed, but I wasn't going to ask for forgiveness. It was a lesson to myself. I had to make better choices, better decisions than the ones I made leading up to this fiasco. And life would change, eventually. I would have my day.

Until then, I did have to control my anger. Note to self: Stay in control or something else will slip.

The ladies worked quickly, apologizing for turning on the vacuum which I swished away with my hand.

They had the newspaper, still folded, tucked into my wastebasket, along with the broken plate and glasses. They replaced it with an identical wastebasket, bowed and exited my apartment.

I was famished but refreshed from the shower. It was time for action, but first, I needed to eat.

My CFO for Bone Frog Security was meeting me in an hour, but he'd arrived last night and was staying downtown. I picked up my phone and dialed him.

"Marco," he said. "I hope we're still on for—"

"Change of plans. This will be a breakfast meeting. Downstairs, in the dining room here at the Towers. I'm headed there now, so anytime you want to show up works for me."

"I was just about to step into the shower, so I'll be over in about fifteen minutes."

"That'll be fine."

The dull pause and heavy breathing on the other end of the line told me Frank Goodman felt apprehensive about the meeting. I knew he'd been sending his resume out, thinking that my change in financial fortune might cause me to cut back on non-essential personnel. It always amazed me how people could self-sort for a downsize. It hadn't been what I had planned to discuss today. But his behavior got my attention.

"Did you bring the reports I asked for?"

"Of course, Marco. It's quite a lot to digest."

"I'll bet." Fuckin Rebecca was good at looting. She was good at everything, including fucking me senseless. I hoped she would be a very sore loser, because it would be so much more pleasurable for me to watch her total meltdown. I wanted her destruction to be a public, ruthless event so that no one ever considered doing such a thing to me again. Yes, I knew that made me a hard man. But it also would make me bullet-proof.

"Well, Marco, see you in a few." His voice wavered with nervousness.

"Yes. You. Will. And by the way, will you join me for a Breakfast in Boston? It's some specialty drink the bartender makes here. I'm going to try one and want you to join me."

"Whatever you like, Marco."

"And I understand the bacon is specially cured, comes direct from a hog farm in Nebraska, too."

"Marco—I don't—"

"Oh, that's right. You eat Kosher."

"I try. If there is a reason I am to eat bacon, like are you considering purchasing a meat packing plant, I can justify some things, but…"

"No. Bacon for the greasy goodness of the fat sizzling in the pan. That kind of hickory-smoked bacon. I'll enjoy it alone, then. But you can drink."

"Yes, I can. But I usually—"

"Today is a new day, Frank. We're going to do a lot of things differently from now on. We have a lot of territory to cover, and the enemy has had a head start on us."

"Exactly. That's the Marco I knew would show up. And I'm greatly relieved to see it too, sir. We're taking no prisoners, is that right?" The timbre of his voice didn't match his words, but they were good words, nonetheless. It meant he was trying to keep up.

"You've got it. I hope you have the taste for war."

Frank didn't answer that one, which bothered me a little. I knew he wasn't a wartime CFO, but he was an excellent forensic accountant, which had been his job as a department head at the IRS for nearly twenty years before he joined my firm.

"See you shortly, Marco."

I scanned the cityscape, following cars traveling along the seaboard. This wasn't the commercial or shipping district more for tourists. A few regular sport fishing outfits and even a pirate ship for roaring drunken parties were docked and sparsely attended. Tugboats and tour ferries crammed into the harbor too. A steady stream of delivery trucks and caterers worked along the docks. A couple stainless steel breakfast burrito trucks honked and attracted workers from the nearby warehouses.

After one last check in the mirror, I headed down-stairs, ready to do battle. It might have been my imagination, but I thought I could smell faint traces of her scent lingering still in the elevator. I guessed I was only the second or third person to use it after her early morning departure. It was nice lace on an otherwise steel-cut day.

I nodded to the bartender. He motioned me over.

"Everything okay? Was something not to your liking, Mr. Gambini?"

"No. It was the headline that bothered me some. Nothing to do with you."

"I want you to know I will re-create that breakfast for you if you'll take a seat."

"I'm meeting a colleague in the dining room. Make it two, but hold the bacon on his. And two Breakfast in Bostons please."

"You got it. Just have them seat you and I'll be right over with the drinks. And the envelope—do you need duplicate information? I can get another copy for you, if you need it."

"Yes, that will be good. Sealed again, like the first time."

"Yessir. Coming right up."

He spread his hand, palm up, out over the bar and Marco followed his direction to the small dining room. Even at nine in the morning, the lighting was dimmed and intimate.

Within minutes my refreshed Breakfast in Boston drink was sitting in front of me. Just as my biscuits and jam arrived, Frank Goodman walked into the dining room with his black briefcase in tow. I'd always thought he was a good-looking guy hiding behind those big glasses. He dressed so conservatively, nobody ever remembered him. I wondered what would make a man do that to himself.

He sat across the table from me, set his case on his knees and flipped open the brass locking devices with two loud clicks, releasing the top.

"Frank, Frank. Let's eat first. I'm sure we can delve into all the financials after we get something in our bellies," I said, stopping him.

He was flummoxed for just a second.

"It's going to be bad news, anyway. Have some biscuits, coffee, and this drink is to die for. A little orange juice and alcohol is needed to digest this stuff, right?"

He pushed his horn-rimmed glasses back on his nose, closed the case and tucked it beside his ankles under the table.

"Very well." He took his lay of the table, draped his lap with a linen napkin, chose a fluffy biscuit, and covered it with soft whipped cream cheese. Then he added blackberry jam.

"Really? Cream cheese and jam?" I asked him.

He hesitated before depositing the entire top half of the biscuit in his enormous mouth but smiled with lips closed as he consumed the warm delight, nodding. Covering his mouth, my CFO mumbled.

"Excuse me, Mr. Gambini, but it isn't often you get whipped cream cheese. I thought it could be butter at first, which would have worked just as well. Trust me, the combination is outstanding, assuming you don't have a hockey puck for a biscuit. These are fabulous."

I could barely understand him.

"They are," I said, matching his combination. "And I agree with your choice. I'm hooked on something new."

"No doubt you'll work it out in the gym later. I'll just keep adding it to my pregnancy," he said, patting his small but developing paunch.

The brew was not as pleasant as my Black Rifle coffee upstairs, but with the cream, was acceptable. I made a mental note to inform them I'd like the Towers to support my Veteran-owned coffee company friends.

"How was your trip up, Frank?"

"My dad used to take a room at the Seaton Arms years ago when he wanted to get away on business. But I think he really wanted to get away from my mom and all us kids. God knows what he was up to there. It was like deja-vu staying there last night. I thought I could even smell his old cigar smoke."

"Your father was a good man, Frank. As you know, he was one of my first investors. In those days, it meant a lot too."

"He was. And I miss him, that's for sure. I'm a better businessman today because of all his yelling and prodding he gave me over the years. He never liked that I worked for the IRS, until he had a big audit himself. And then he accused me of orchestrating it so he'd get off my back. But in the end, we both weathered the storm. He drilled that entrepreneurial spirit into me and trained out the wild side somehow. He was right. Made me a better man. You remind me a little of him, sir."

"Please, Frank, we are the same age. Don't call me sir. It makes me feel old, and I don't need to be reminded I'm not in my twenties. It's been how many years now? Let's not be that formal."

"No, I understand. Just showing some respect and wanted you to know how grateful I am to have a job with Bone Frog."

I figured that was a little cover his ass in case I knew about the resumes being sent out. He was smarter than he looked sometimes.

"Duly noted."

He finished off his Breakfast in Boston, and our waiter asked if he wanted another. He put up his palm, no, before checking in with me. He asked for scrambled eggs on the side, and watched as oatmeal was delivered to me, covered in strawberries.

"Wait. I'll have one of those," he changed his mind, pointing to my bowl.

"Very well, sir," the waiter answered and left without a sound.

"I slept like a baby last night. How about you, Marco?"

I smiled, but my stomach gurgled and my groin got hard just thinking about the delightful romp I'd had.

But right now I had raw meat between my teeth and I was ready to tear apart the animal who had caused me pain. Now wasn't the time for screwing or rising to new heights of pleasure. Now was the time for getting bloody, preparing for combat. I always carried my Glock, even when I was in cities where guns were outlawed. I had every license and clearance known to man to conceal carry. It would be like showing up naked to a cocktail party not to have my favorite sidearm, which had been with me longer than even my former wife.

We completed our breakfast and the table was cleared. Frank opened his briefcase and placed a sheaf of papers in front of me. Some were reports. Some were graphs attached to supporting documents. One was a subpoena.

"What's this?" I said, holding it up between my thumb and two fingers like it was a piece of dirty laundry.

"Came in last night just before I was leaving the office. By courier."

"Nice touch. Just before you're to come report to me. Who leaked?"

"I think it was a coincidence, really. Your gal, Jennifer, seemed very surprised."

I glanced at the cover page. It was an order to appear and bring records, at Rebecca's attorney's office.

"When it comes to Rebecca, there are no coincidences," I said. "She shits on a timetable. I don't think she's been surprised since that fuck, she got at her daddy's horse ranch when she gave her virginity up to a man she thought was a crown prince who turned out to be a royal con man instead."

"Wow."

"Oh, don't be surprised. She grew up hard. Not a lot of love in that home."

"Well, that's harsh. I mean, sorry for her."

"She'd slit your throat if she heard you say that, so be careful."

Frank adjusted his tie, touching his neck right where the knife would go in smoothly for the kill, and looked at me warily. "Marco, you're going to have to make some tough decisions. What they're asking about is your construction project in Florida—the veteran-ownership venture, building homes for injured vets"

"Bone Frog Development. The Trident Towers project."

"Exactly."

"Makes perfect sense. She'd want to hit me where it hurt the most. Odd that she would go for a non-profit like that. I don't expect to make a dime. I'll probably lose my shirt on it. Why the hell would they care about that?"

"You're asking me? You were married to her. Anything I've heard would be just gossip."

I pushed the papers forward and leaned back in my chair, folding my hands together over my chest. Now we were getting to the good stuff. The truth.

"Try me."

"Excuse me?" His eyes were wide and his glasses slipped down his nose, needing to be pushed back again. From years of interrogating bad guys and judging tribal leaders as to whether or not they could be trusted, I saw the dilation in his pupils, along with a slight worry line crop up between his eyebrows. He knew he got caught.

"What have you heard? Spill it, Frank."

When a subject looks down at his hands with fingers locked together, I knew he was looking for a way out, a friendly hand to give him a solution to wiggle free.

He was out of luck.

I'd already been told he was saying to others he doubted I would survive the coming months. This was about whether or not I could trust him. I didn't begrudge his opinions, but I damn sure better get the truth to a direct ask. This was his chance to keep his job, if he still wanted it.

"I'm a numbers guy, Marco," he said as he raised his gaze to meet mine. He was fortunate he didn't look away as he spoke his truth. "I've seen all these things coming and going, and you're going to have a huge cash flow problem in a few months. All these audits and attorneys' fees are drying up your liquid, not to mention the settlements you've agreed to. And the public comments in the news, well, I've been asked by several people if they should start looking for work elsewhere. And, although I haven't heard it directly, some have said that the contracts have started to dry up. You know how the government works. They don't like controversy."

"Even though they specialize in it."

He kept his eyes locked on mine, thankfully. "Exactly. But even you have to admit, the numbers don't lie."

I leaned forward, placing my palms on the table, and then grabbed the paperwork to start reading over the fine print. I wasn't going to tell him not to worry, because he was right. The numbers were worse than I thought. I was going to have to study these and then give clear direction.

"Where would you suggest I begin?" I asked.

"I'd sell off one of the entities. The airline, the shipping company, or the leasing agency. I'd boost your personnel security contracts since they are the most lucrative, and frankly, they are the most vulnerable. You might consider using some of your sales to hire a Washington PR company."

"I've never had one before. You think it's wise to do that now? Start a new project?"

He shrugged. "You need to protect your personal connections with your higher ups. You need those contracts. It's the fuel that makes everything else run smoothly. Your friendship with the Vice President, the Secretary of State—you need to make sure they are solid."

He was right. I needed to reassure myself things were that bad, first.

"And," Frank started, placing his hands on the table. "I know you've never considered this, but it would be a good idea to cultivate some contracts with the Kingdoms."

"No. No non-US."

"But Clearwater and Red Dog are making big inroads into that," he argued.

"You don't know their numbers, Frank, or do you?"

"No, sir—Marco. I don't. I have nothing to go by except what I see in the papers, and the contract bulletins."

"And you don't know the casualties they are suffering, do you?"

"No, Marco."

"They put their men and women in bad places. I

won't do that. I don't care how bad ass we are. I won't do that."

He leaned back in the chair, and I knew there was something else.

"What is it?"

"Yesterday, I got a call from Senator Campbell. He asked me point blank if you were interested in meeting with a delegation from the Kingdom of Bonin. They have just signed on to bankroll a housing project in North Africa. They are going to need security for their royal family as they negotiate and follow-up on these projects."

"So? I'll meet with them, but I've never had to take one of those jobs before. I usually collect a referral fee and send it to someone else."

"I understand, but Senator Campbell said he was hesitant to refer them to you. He had questions. He asked me if your recent setbacks had caused you to lose your nerve."

I was ready to toss the paperwork, the table and all four chairs out the large window overlooking the bustling street outside.

Hadn't Frank ever heard the term, "Don't shoot the messenger?"

CHAPTER 4

Shannon

I WAITED TWO days before flying home to St. Pete. My body still rumbled—shaking, really, from the insides of my core all the way to my toes. I'd stepped into forbidden territory, yet something was so satisfying about it, I was a moth to the flame. It might destroy me, but I'd accomplished what I set out to do, and now, unexpectedly, I wanted more. So much more.

After Emily's death, Mom and Dad moved to Florida once I left for college a few years later. They joined an active adult community in order to fill that horrible void left with Em's passing. I was grateful the burden didn't fall on me, because I was also reeling from my older sister's untimely death. Those were strange years, finishing up high school and then applying to colleges with as much direction as a rudderless boat. The house had been so quiet without her. My mother rarely smiled, and my dad drank more. Never one for many words anyway, he retreated into a darkness that was so black it threatened to take me with it.

I became invisible. I never knew how much light Emily shed on our family until that radiance was extinguished. I was careful not to upset my parents, and they tried very hard to shield me from the hurt and pain they were feeling and could not help but show. It was a standoff with no winners.

I finished my degree in California, at Sonoma State, in communications and started exploring my options for future television work, which had been my long-term goal. I learned how to look and act professionally and took on an acting coach. A small low-budget indie film even cast me, giving me screen credits only. I modeled some, but when I was encouraged to go to near-starvation levels to get my weight down, and I refused. Plus-sized jobs started booking me, even though I was normal weight. My self-esteem plummeted and at my lowest, had an affair with my drama teacher in college. That lasted until his marriage broke up over his affair with another student.

I vowed that would never happen again to me. It was not a part of my life I felt very proud of. Lesson learned.

But it whetted my appetite for older men.

Em would have married Marco Gambini if she hadn't been killed in that car accident that took her life with three of her sorority sisters'. My mother and I had hoped the accident would curtail my father's drinking, because the drunk who hit them walked away with just a broken nose. He got some jail time, but not enough to satisfy our revenge and anger.

And that brought the other heartache into my life. Marco Gambini, my older sister's fiancé, was my imaginary lover, my girl-crush, the man I compared every other man to when I dated. I guess he could even be considered a father figure since my father became a mere ghost, albeit a ghost who played golf every day and liked to sit and watch my mother play Bunko and Pinochle. After the funeral, I never saw Marco again, until two days ago when I walked into the Bachelor Towers, took up a seat, and became my sister for one whole night. It was a gift to myself, something I think Em would have approved of if I'd had the ability to ask her. I needed to know I could play for keeps with a man like that.

I walked away knowing that it didn't work that way. He wasn't a man like that. He was the only man in the universe for me. My teenage radar had been spot on. He was a keeper.

Now I had a problem.

So when Marco didn't call, I knew I had to go back to the beach retreat I'd purchased with my own savings, the little one-bedroom place painted bright yellow with turquoise trim, nestled in the bluffs overlooking the white sugar-sand beach of the Florida gulf coast.

Some might judge me, and they should be careful. I've never been the girl to resurrect my dead sister's life to make it my own. That's not me. I needed to revive my own life, not Em's. Sort of my right of passage.

Call it my empathetic nature, but I knew I could help heal his wounds, temporarily. For one night. For one night, I could pretend that the confluence of events between us had never happened. That we had no history. I wasn't looking for a future. I was looking to bury the past once and for all.

Everything about him was familiar. His scent, the way he smiled, kissed. The way his fingers explored. The little grunts and deep grumbles in his chest, even his whispers and sighs as I rose for him, bloomed for him, showed him my insides—that place I'd never shown anyone else. Oh, I wasn't a virgin, by any means. But I was new to love, to what Em had in her life. I had begged for just one taste of him, and now I would be tainted forever.

Did it bother me he never called me back?

I didn't expect it. I suspected he wouldn't.

Would I try to chase him, duplicate that night of passion again?

I told myself that, no, that wasn't the agreement I'd made with my better angels. With Em. With him, even though he was completely unaware of it.

Did I expect he'd recognize Em in my eyes?

I wasn't sure, but I'd hoped not. They were my eyes needing his examination and determined lovemaking. It was my body he pleasured, that I gave to him. It was for and about me. And I would be forever grateful, even as the remembrance of that night would leave me breathless, haunted, and wet for weeks. Possibly months or even years. I might never find that intensity again. But there was one ground rule I would never break.

I would never chase him. I found him. One time. Now it would be up to him and only him, to go beyond that. As my female parts recovered from the long night of lovemaking, the ache inside remained.

Only way to deal with it was to call it delicious, ra-re, and tuck it away in my wine cellar of experiences where it would remain a vintage release consumed sparingly.

After all, a good wine was meant to be enjoyed, not stored forever. That's exactly what I did.

THE TAMPA INTERNATIONAL Airport was a dose of reality that came on me like a firehose. Retirees flocked in groups as tour operators collected them all with brightly colored guide signs held high above their heads. Families were reunited. Young couples arrived to join the throngs at the Gulf Coast beaches. Businessmen in suits sweated under the heat, unaccustomed to the humidity. Children ran around everywhere, and pets were released from their crates.

I passed long lines of passengers waiting to escape from the Florida sun or begin their trip home after a vacation. It was a bustling society of everyone coming from and heading to different places, and for a moment in time, all residing within the confines of the terminals spilling out into the hot parking garages or hotel passenger vans.

I retrieved my one bag, then found my car in long term parking, and headed for the refuge of the coast.

My shoulders relaxed the closer I got to the water's edge. Just before I arrived at Beach Trail Road and the driveway leading up to my little beach bungalow, my phone rang.

"Judie. I'm back, almost at the house. How has everything been?"

My best friend reminded me so much of my big sister Emily, it was uncanny. She had been the one who found Marco's headlines and placed those news printouts on my desk in my cubby.

"You know, sunny with a chance of rain. They hired and fired a new intern..."

"Already? That's got to be a record."

"I think so. Apparently, her dress attire was not appropriate. It got her the job, but it's what got her fired."

"Oh, I get it now. Clarence."

Clarence Thompson was our evening anchor personality, complete with hair plugs and makeup, even when he wasn't on the air. He was getting long in the tooth, with habits that weren't aging well with the female population at TMBC. It was only a matter of time before he'd be forced out by a sexual harassment lawsuit. But this train wreck of a man just couldn't keep his hands and his mouth under control.

"Fucking Clarence. The cat that ate the canary."

"The one and only. So, Shannon, mission accomplished? Did you meet him?"

I hadn't told her everything I was planning, and now I was glad I hadn't.

"Yup. He's still as handsome as I remember. A real gentleman, too," I lied.

I could still hear the words he growled over me, "I love fucking you." My badge of honor. I nearly came in my car seat just recalling how he commanded my body while I was powerless to refuse him anything. In my mind I told him to fuck me harder, take me from behind, from the side, upside down if he wanted to. I could still feel his grip on my hips almost to the point of bruising, clutching me tight as he skillfully drilled me a new meaning of the word *fuck.*

I checked my rear-view mirror as I pulled into my

driveway.

Yup, I had perspiration on my upper lip. Good thing Judie couldn't see the flush on my cheeks too.

"So did you tell him who you were?"

"Not on your life."

"So that's it? You met him, what, and then walked away?"

I saw myself hanging off the bed as he buried his face in my crotch. I could feel the smooth grey carpet with my fingertips, my back arched, my knees bent and spread wide for him. I didn't walk away. I *floated* away. I vibrated all the way down the elevator. If I'd bumped into anyone, we would have both burst into flames, with how hot I was.

"Yes, I met him, and left my phone number. If he wants to see me, he'll call. But the next step is up to him. I just wanted to meet him and not have him feel obligated to talk to me because of Em. And he didn't figure it out. Like I said, he was a real gentleman."

I had him in my mouth as his fingers lazily messed my hair in all directions. I pretended to hear him whisper, "Oh, sweetheart," which of course didn't really happen. But I got him harder again after our second or third round, and he showed his appreciation thoroughly afterwards.

"You surprise me, Shannon. From all the talk—"

"What do you take me for, Judie?"

Again, my lies were making me a bit careless. But I couldn't help thinking he'd recognize the scent of my body, too, if I were to casually pass him by in some hallway. That he'd be moved to slip me into a broom closet or bathroom for something dangerous and quick.

I was every bit the slut she was thinking of. I was desperate to prove it too.

No, something had been unleashed, and things were never going to be the same again. But that had been what I was looking for all along. I walked around like a marionette, my wrists and ankles tied with invisible golden threads pulling me back to Boston where I would watch the twinkle lights of the city until I could no longer focus.

Judie paused. "You're kinda breathing hard, Shannon. Are you okay?"

"Never better."

CHAPTER 5

Marco

I TOOK TWO days, reviewing the numbers carefully, and could see how Frank would come to the conclusion I needed to unload one of my entities in order to save the rest. My net worth was *less* than half what it had been before the divorce and resulting proceedings, something I hadn't wanted to look at in black and white until now, but the biggest problem was that my much-needed cash flow had been consumed with legal fees and other restructuring necessary to protect me and the rest of my assets. All that would be on-going. And now she wanted the Florida project, the one entity that wasn't going to make me money, but was the one thing I felt the most passionately about: getting homes for disabled Navy SEALs.

I scoured the balance sheets, searched my records for details he'd given me online, backing up the summaries he'd presented. I looked for a flaw in his analysis.

I didn't find one.

As I'd learned from my training, I began coming up with a plan by first filling out the knowns and identifying the huge gaps and unknowns before coming up with the plan I could dive feet first into. The list was growing the more I brainstormed. Prioritizing the most important, I began checking off the items as fast as I could re-allocate them, sometimes even changing their value. We used to do this all the time on the Teams, checking and re-checking targets and assets, evaluating and re-evaluating methods and task details. A successful mission was all about identifying the strategy needed so we wouldn't have to think—we could just execute the plan. And all of it was always heavily dependent on the quality of the information used to create the plan in the first place. That's what I was going for. Accuracy. Facts. Looking for problems and potential pitfalls so nothing would be unaccounted for.

I spoke to several department heads and called a board meeting in D.C. for early next week, when I hoped to have a decision made so I could announce our new direction. I needed to touch base with my attorney about the new subpoena. I toyed with the idea of flying down to Florida to meet with the non-profit group working on the housing project, just to take their temperature and perhaps warn them.

The comment Senator Campbell made bothered me, and I knew shirking that phone call would be a mistake. My heart and my gut weren't up to it, but I manned up and dialed his personal number.

"Hey, Marco. Long time no hear. You still got all your arms and legs intact?"

I had been trained never to show emotion, so, even on the phone I wasn't going to wince because I knew he'd hear it in my voice.

"I picked her for all the wrong reasons, Senator. Thing is, I can admit a mistake when I've made one, and this one was colossal. But not fatal. You know what they say about a wounded bear?"

Campbell had a belly laugh at that one. "Glad to say I don't share your experience, Marco, knock on wood. Beth and I have been happily married for nearly twenty-four years." He paused carefully, taking in a deep breath. "Frank told me about your meeting on Tuesday, and he mentioned he brought up my offer to make introductions to the sultan of Bonin. He said you might consider speaking with him."

"I am willing to listen. No promises."

"Of course. I think he's been around long enough to understand this. But he is rather persistent and insisted that the two of you discuss your mutual futures *in person.*"

I suspected the sultan was a heavy contributor to the senator's re-election campaign. Whatever mutual future there was between the sultan and I would no doubt include the senator as well.

"As I said, no promises. But yes, I'll speak with him."

"Good. That's good, Marco. I know you are busy, but when can I tell him you'd be available and are you willing to travel?"

It would be far easier for me to travel with a small contingent than for the sultan to come with his harem, his princelings and several of his grandchildren. I could slip in and out easier than he ever could, so our meeting could truly be done in secret. I agreed to let the senator arrange a meeting at one of the sultan's properties, a luxurious palace on one of the islands in the Indian Ocean. Once when I was still on the Teams, we had helped with a sweep of the grounds when a suspected terrorist was smuggled there. We captured the bastard in a storage closet inside sultan's enormous kitchen. The terrorist saved us a lot of time and trouble, too, since his interrogation was done in secret aboard a Naval vessel nearby.

I could arrange the transportation, thereby ensuring my safety, if the sultan could agree to the airdrop and the exact timing. Senator Campbell promised to get back to me within twenty-four hours. I asked him for permission to use Naval assets if need be for landing and he said he'd arrange it.

Checking contract scheduling, I noticed I had Little Bird, my pet nickname for one of my favorite little Sikorskys, safely stored in the Maldives. That might give me some luck with Diego Garcia friendlies, and besides, the Navy owed me some serious favors. If I could piggyback, an Indian Ocean meeting was entirely possible and wouldn't require much in the way of expense.

So I was boxing myself in, fixing myself up not to be able to say no, since Senator Campbell had some enviable Armed Services creds. But more importantly, his wife was the younger sister of the First Lady, which had even more weight.

Barely four hours went by before I was contacted by "Harry", the sultan's gay bastard son, born of a favorite harem girl and never in line to the throne, partly because of his birth lineage but most certainly due to his sexual preferences. I'd worked with him before. He'd grown up as close to an American kid as possible, even attended NYU film school while living with his mother in a purchased brownstone in Brooklyn Heights. The sultan hired him right out of college to be his social secretary and trusted the kid with his life. In return, the son lived a lavish lifestyle he'd have never had and promised he'd never disrespect his father.

"Well, Marco, I guess we'll be working together again. My father is most anxious to get caught up."

"I'll bet. So, which one of your idiot brothers is heading the project in Africa?" I asked. Harry, short for Hanarabi, and I had always been on close terms, not dissimilar to how I used to joke with my Teammates.

"Oh, that would be Khalil and Absalom. You know they both graduated with advanced degrees in engineering and architecture at MIT."

"How many buildings did that cost the sultan?"

"No, I think there might have been some help, but they earned it on their own, with some extra tutoring, of course. But it was earned fair and square, just how you like it."

I got the dig about me being the square one, but let it go. I didn't like the joke, but he had to put up with a lot of stuff from me in the past, too.

"Glad to hear it. I was afraid they'd be tossed before they could finish."

"Hardly, Uncle Marco," Harry resurrected the name I'd not heard for over five years. "They were way more serious about their studies and their legacy than I ever was. I'm still looking to make my directorial debut."

"Which means your father has turned you down another dozen times."

"Quite right. He isn't into a gay West Side Story." He sighed. "But in the meantime, all this work takes the place of the bright lights on the marquee in Times Square. Someday, if my father doesn't manage to live to be a hundred like his father, I might actually get a chance!"

"In his line of work, that's a good thing, Harry."

"You mean being sultan?"

"I know men who would consider it a full-time job to keep all those women happy in your father's stable. And I mean him no disrespect, Harry."

"Oh, I get it. But he pays to play. Look at all the family he supports. So now he wants to see my brothers become successful businessmen, something he was not allowed to do by his own father."

"Do they know?"

"Do they know what? Oh! That I am their brother? Oh heaven's no! There are always palace rumors, but nothing he can't quickly quash. My mother's life would be in danger, and she has no protection."

"So he's still kept that golden leash on you."

"Oh, Marco, you know I love the man. He's always been good to us. I am a devoted sycophant, and he knows he can trust me with his life. I don't think he'd say the same about any of his wives."

"Bingo. Women are complicated. I learned that lesson the hard way."

"I've heard."

I knew they'd have done their research before reaching out. "So you have the dates and the arrangements figured out?"

"I have them coming to you over a secure link, encrypted with your mother's birthdate added to the date of your wedding."

"Grrr..." They really had stepped up their game.

"Oh, stop it, Uncle Marco. She can't be *that* bad. You were with her for a long time."

"Too long. Tell me she hasn't made any contact with him."

"Haven't heard a peep. So you'll be coming alone or is there a new Mrs. Gambini in the wings?"

"I'm solo. Probably going to be that way for the remainder."

"So we're more alike than you realized, Uncle Marco."

"Watch it, kid."

We wrapped up, and several minutes later I got the encrypted files giving me the time, place and several letters of permission and introduction to any of the government entities I might have to deal with to travel.

At the bottom of the document was a figure the sultan was offering, which I knew I could bump up if I needed to. But it was a figure that would pay for all my business expenses for the next three years.

I smiled, not at the number, but at the idea that I didn't have to share one penny of that with Rebecca.

If I took the job, of course.

CHAPTER 6

Shannon

THE NEWSROOM BUZZED with local discussions and issues related to voter registration and challenges to politicians running in various runoff elections and pivots for posturing in the next general election, which was thankfully several months away. Of course, weather was more important as residents of the greater Tampa area and beach communities planned their vacations, their fishing trips and outdoor events.

I allowed the makeup artist to finish, curling my hair and doing a soft blowout, when I removed the drape and stepped into the green screen. I demonstrated that the next hurricane would be heading west of us, heading right up the middle of the Gulf to land perhaps on New Orleans or Galveston, and not anywhere near my sleepy beach bungalow. I gracefully pointed to the string of "recruits" as I called them, lined up to run in and wreak havoc right behind Hurricane Eloise.

Everyone was praying that Eloise would change her temperament and become a tropical storm. I told my audience that I was hoping she'd be a good girl, and winked. The Program Director gave me a wide smile in return, followed by a thumbs up.

Of course, I couldn't get off the stage fast enough to avoid bumping into Clarence Thompson, who pretended he didn't see me. It gave him a change to feel my tits with the flabby upper chest of his. If his hands had been used to stop his forward momentum, I was prepared to slap him. Hard.

Luckily, Clarence was creepy, but somewhat on his better behavior. Besides, there were ten sets of eyes staring right at both of us.

"Shannon, glad you made it back to our beautiful little paradise. How was Boston?"

I was surprised he knew anything about where I was going.

"Colder," I said, making sure it sounded that way too.

He blushed pink from my subtle insult and then broke out in a wide smile. "Well, we're all very glad you're back. Things are just never the same when you're gone." He had placed his palm over his heart. He should have just been honest and grabbed his dick.

I imagined the scent, the feel of Marco's strong body on top of me, beneath my undulating hips, and how he made me feel. I took secret pride in the knowledge that this cretin couldn't take any of that beautiful memory away from me. It would forever be my secret, the most valuable thing I owned, at least for right now.

I ignored the comment and walked back to the green room for something to drink, awaiting my next performance. The room was plastered with big screens—which not only showed the content of tonight's broadcast in three sizes, but several other news channels'. The mix of national and cable kept us current.

One of the stories a competing station showed was on the housing project Marco Gambini had started in Belleair Beach and how there was some concern the project would no longer be built, due to complications resulting from Marco's recent financial setbacks, without mentioning the contentious divorce. I walked closer to the screen with my water bottle as the newscaster played a quick clip of Rebecca Gambini's interview done earlier that day. I observed the woman with new appreciation for what a mismatch she was for him, and it made me smile.

"Yes, well, there have been some restructuring measures taking place at the present time. Some of the Bone Frog Industries projects have been sadly neglected, and I'm rushing in to see what I can do to rescue them," she said, her lying eyes trying to look all wide and doe-like. I knew exactly what kind of poison brewed in her belly, and I said a secret prayer that those acids would become lethal.

The interviewer asked her a question. "Forgive me, but wasn't this a project your former husband had been working on alone? So now you've been given authority to carry the ball, so to speak?"

Rebecca clearly didn't like that comment and glared at the young interviewer. She throttled the microphone placed toward her, squeezed her fingers over the young woman's, leaned in, and said, "It's called *fruits of the marriage*, Gaylee. I'm passionate about this work and how it is to go forward, so that's why I'm here." She outstretched her many-ringed and diamond-encrusted fingers with the bright red nail polish, motioning over the vacant lot that had five acres of palm trees cut down behind her.

The woman was here! She was in this area, spreading her venom all around her. I shouldn't have been surprised.

This gave me an idea.

MY PROGRAM DIRECTOR, Jared Newsome, was shutting down his office when I arrived after my third weather report. His warm, handsome face didn't hide his appreciation that I'd graced his doorway.

"All done tonight?"

"You know I am."

He shrugged. "Care to join me for a cocktail? You can tell me about your trip."

Why was everyone at the station riveted on my personal life?

"No, thanks. I appreciate it, but I'm going to lay low for a few days and get my land legs back. I really don't like flying."

"Really?" He gave me a quick look over and then shut his eyes tight. "I'm sorry. That was—"

"What I would have thought too," I answered for him. "And no, it's not a sexual thing like they say. I'm just tired from the travel and being jammed into small spaces. I always get this way when I come back from a trip."

"Of course. So what's up?" He closed his laptop, pushed it into his padded case, tucked his rolling chair into his desk, and came around to stand in front of me. I could tell he was going to ask me again, and again I would be turning him down. But I liked him. I genuinely liked him, and I was hoping that we could maintain the good friendship and trust I felt we had together. I considered him sort of a mentor. "You've not been looking for greener pastures, have you?"

Now I understood his concern. He was wondering if I'd interviewed at the larger Boston market. It would be an obvious step-up in my career, although perhaps a bit soon.

"No, Jared. You don't have to worry about anything like that. I'm extremely grateful for everything you're doing for me here at the station. I'm not looking."

Well, it wasn't a lie. I wasn't looking for a new job, at least.

"Okay, that's a relief. We think you fit in nice here. We'd certainly hope you feel the same way."

"I do, Jared."

"Clarence isn't bothering you too much, I hope."

"You don't have to worry about that. If he comes on to me, I know how get rid of him, as I've continually done since I started. I don't blame him, even though you know I don't like him very much. He's wired up wrong. He's like a dog you want to rescue but he keeps biting the hand that feeds him. He's his own worst enemy, and I honestly don't think he'll stop until he does something big."

"Very astute and mature of you, Shannon."

"He's *your* problem, Jared."

"So we aren't going to have a drink, Clarence is minding himself for now. You aren't looking for a job. Why are we talking here?"

He was good at getting right down to things. That gave me courage.

"You know I've always wanted to do more things related to the news, not just weather. And I have a couple of ideas about stories I'd like to pursue, with your permission. I don't want to give up my weather duties, but I'd like to tackle a real news story."

I could see he was intrigued. His eyes sparkled as he studied my face. I found it difficult to look him straight in the eyes because I wanted this so bad. Finally I looked up and decided to just go for it. All he could say was no, anyway.

"I watched in the green room about Rebecca Gambini's trip out here to assume duties related to the Navy SEAL housing project that was proposed at Belleair Beach. I think I could do a kickass interview of the woman, her plans, and her position on this. It has a lot of human interest, not only because of the divorce but the need for housing for these Navy heroes. Plus, this project would impact the local economy. It has all the earmarks of a series of special reports. I'd like to help her champion it a little bit."

Jared rolled back on his heels. I could tell he'd never considered this coming from my mouth.

"You've really thought about this, haven't you?"

"I have."

"Do you have any special insight?" His eyes looked unremarkably calm so I didn't suspect anything Judie and I had discussed. I decided to deflect a bit.

"I might need your introduction to her. I don't know her. But I think she'd like another story. The last interviewer got several things wrong, and I can tell she perhaps offended the woman. I don't think I would do that."

I hoped that my insides didn't give me away. And I really had no ulterior motive with the interviews. I was just a moth to the flame, powerless to walk away from an opportunity, even though my better judgment was nudging me in the gut. I didn't care. I had to try this, just like I had to meet Marco after all these years. I just couldn't stay away, seeing as how she flew right into my neighborhood as if it had been predestined.

"You might have something there, Shannon. I agree that there's a story under all that drama. Made for someone with some considerable journalistic chops, though. Are you sure you want to step into the fire pit?"

"Are you saying you don't think I can handle it?"

"Oh, I think you could handle the interview well enough. But I'm wondering how you'll handle Clarence or some of the other groupies trying to claw their way up the ladder. You could become part of the story, you know, if it doesn't go well. Are you prepared to become part of the drama? Really?"

I was shaking, brimming with excitement. He was at the edge of letting me do what I'd dreamt of doing.

Was this really happening?

"I'll say you warned me. But one thing is for sure. If it goes badly, you'll not only have a weather girl, you'd have somewhat of a celebrity. How bad would that be for ratings?"

Jared chuckled, studying his shoes.

"Shannon, I wish you'd let me buy you a drink..."

"No."

"You'd give up this chance?"

"I won't do it for a drink with you. That's not how I work. If it's no, it's no. If it's yes, then it's a solid, no-holds-barred yes."

I watched the softness in his eyes, the way he licked his lips and studied mine. He wanted me. I didn't shirk from showing him I knew. But the answer was still no. Sure, I could cajole him, have a good time and make myself believe I could convince him with my sexual prowess. Then he'd pretend he hadn't lost all respect for me, just like he'd lost any respect for any other woman to take advantage that way. And he'd hate himself too. And me.

It would be easy with him, because he was attractive and he wasn't begging, just leaving the door open. But I wanted more than that. I wanted the chance to earn something on my terms. I wanted to prove to myself, to the part of Em that still lingered all around me, that I was ready to step into the real world. I could sing at the top of my lungs, a full-on opera singer who had hidden her talent.

It was time to take the gloves off.

"Then it's a yes. God help me, Shannon, but I believe in you. If it doesn't work out, then can we have that drink?" He winked at me, standing a little too close.

"Ask me when it's over, Jared. Don't ask me now."

"Okay, then. I'll make some calls and see if I can get you an interview. Go prove me a discoverer of brilliant talent, Shannon. Make me proud. Take that brass ring all the way to the bank. I'll cover where I can, if I'm needed."

"Thank you." I could have kissed him easily.

I gave him a flirtatious smile instead and slipped out of his office and back into the bullpen where I could breathe at last.

ALL THE WAY home, my body buzzed. I listened to country music then switched it to New Age then classical. I held my head high, and imagined the To Do list I'd stay up half the night to complete. I wanted to list all the questions I'd ask her. I wouldn't mention Marco. I'd wait for her to do it, and then I'd ask for more information.

By the time I reached my bungalow, a worry had slipped into my head. What would I do if Marco saw the interview and remembered me? What would he think about me stalking him in Boston and inserting myself in his affairs in Tampa? If he sought me out, would I even be able to answer that question?

"I don't know," I said out loud.

But then storm clouds began to lift. I was standing on the beach all of a sudden, long after sunset, feeling the glow of what once was. The sky cleared and all that was left was the heat generating from a full moon at my back. I didn't even remember locking my car, unlocking my house, slipping on my sweats and flip flops, and making it outside to the fresh air and the beach. It was almost like I'd floated here.

It felt like a crossroads, a point of no return.

Was Em behind all this, weaving a tale and cinching me down with those golden cords of hers? Was this her way of living inside my body somehow while he pleasured me? It was ridiculous for me to consider.

It was even more ridiculous to doubt that there wasn't some sentient being out there making it all happen.

Maybe I better start going back to church.

CHAPTER 7

Marco

MY ADMINISTRATIVE TEAM readied for the big meeting in D.C. that was to come in just two days. I informed who would be accompanying me to the Pink Pasha, the sultan's palace on his private island, and we discussed logistics and security issues. Ryan would travel over to inspect the Sikorsky, which hadn't been flown in thirty days and would needed to be re-checked. He'd remain there until our mission details were finalized.

Our online call, which began at four A.M. due to where my team was stationed all over the world, was productive, and we covered a lot of ground. I managed to cross nearly everything off my agenda list, which always brightened my day.

I created a flurry of phone calls, mostly leaving voicemails that would be answered when people arrived at their desks in the US, setting into motion new restructuring plans and reviewing upcoming contracts, bids in the pipeline, contract negotiation procedures and strategies for the next several months. I needed a breather, so I took a break and went for a run.

I always think best while moving, so used this thinking time to get acquainted with the downtown and Harbor areas in Boston. My run through the city was still in the early morning hours before the commute started—my favorite time of day. I returned to my suite, took a shower, dug into more paperwork, and answered phone calls.

Later, I took a late lunch and frequented a couple of favorite haunts I'd been told about and swept through several modern art galleries on my way back to the Towers. I found stimulation in the colorful abstract artwork, my favorite being Italian fusion art glass.

I wanted to plunk down my platinum card, prepared to purchase every piece in that little gallery, since my bare walls at the Towers were driving me crazy. Instead I hesitated, purchasing just one large abstract instead. It reminded me of a woman's nude torso, a sensuous view from the rear. I had a perfect spot for it—right over my bed.

It was everything I could do to stop from having the gallery concierge throw in half a dozen other matching pieces and a bronze I liked to fondle. Being sensitive about my funding dilemma pissed me off, but

I stuffed it back down, planning to use it as fuel for the bonfire I was building under Rebecca's reputation and comfortable lifestyle.

Did that make me a dangerous man?

I hoped so.

One of my Manhattan bankers asked me to stop in at a local Eastern Bank & Trust to review and sign papers, authorizing a transfer of funds that usually happened later in the month. I decided to set it up so that in the future these could happen automatically up to certain limits, but I did wonder why this was coming so soon in the month.

The Bank & Trust office was sterile, just like I found most banks. I remembered the first time I went in to get a loan as a newbie frog. They turned me down—and not nicely, either. Funny thing how banks don't like a lax attitude toward making car payments. That first red Mustang I bought had burned a hole in my credit as fast as it gobbled gas driving up the California coastline in those days.

The next time, a year later, I walked in with Rebecca on my arm. Maybe she was the magic sauce that made it all happen, but that day, we walked out with the promise of being able to buy something in Coronado. It was to be our forever house, until kids.

And that never happened either.

I still owned that house—paid it off in record time.

Oddly enough, she'd left it behind, just like I did with our wedding pictures, in the divorce settlement, almost as if she'd forgotten about it. Since most of my operations were on the East Coast, I didn't use it very often and, instead, had someone run a VRBO, which made some cash that I had stashed in a savings account for a rainy day. Selling that house would net me a cool couple of million, as if that would solve all my financial problems. Otherwise, I'd liquidate it in a heartbeat since the place meant nothing to me.

It was a lush little corner lot with a beach access trail, but no water views. I'd expunged all my memories of how it made me feel to own my first home—to plant palm trees and things in the yard I could go back to in fifty years as an old man and see them standing tall and invincible—just like how I felt at the time.

A little tweak of regret stabbed my stomach as I thought about those days of being drunk on sex and running around being a Boy Scout with my buddies on the Teams. The whole world had been my theater, doing things no one would ever believe, having more fun than I had a right to and coming home to a woman who liked to screw hard and was just as intense as I was. I was a God then, a force for good.

When did it all change? When did life get so dark and difficult?

But I still was that force for good as I left the Teams

and started my passion for business, protecting the innocent and getting paid a lot of money for it. It was just on a larger scale. With more at stake. And solo. Maybe that was how it was supposed to be all along. God sure kicked my butt to remind me I was just a dumb frog at heart. Being a billionaire was just a trapping, an extra piece of equipment to strap on and enjoy for a few moments of my life.

Because that's how it turned out to be. And it would be that way again.

Today, I sort of felt just the same as I did fifteen-plus years ago when I first walked into a bank and got my ass handed to me. No one had to remind me I wasn't in a position of strength and these new "clothes" I was wearing somehow didn't fit to my liking. But I told myself it was only temporary.

Story of my life.

Serena Bolton was the vice president's secretary. She wore a brightly colored yellow and fuchsia dress which belied this time of year in Boston. Her dreadlocks were pulled up on top of her head, woven with yellow satin ribbons, making a striking pattern of rows and zigzags. Occasionally, a tiny pink flower would poke through. Her skin was as dark as the macadam roads I traveled on by taxi, deliciously highlighted with her bright pink lipstick and purple eyeshadow. She resembled one of my Italian fusion glass pieces and was just as lovely to look at.

"Mr. Cullen is waiting for you inside, Mr. Gambini. If you'll just follow me, please."

I sauntered under a large second-story balcony with glass partitioned offices above. She tapped on the vice president's door and I watched my intended target push back his wire rimmed glasses, straighten his jacket, stand, and come to the door. He held out a beefy hand, stubby fingers splayed.

"Mr. Gambini, nice to meet you. Welcome to Boston."

"Thank you, sir," I replied.

He waddled to his seat while motioning to his secretary to return to the lobby area from which we came. He sat down with an audible crunch, directing me to sit across the desk in the single, wooden and very Spartan-looking chair. I noted that most of his meetings were intended to be short and uncomfortable. I girded my loins.

"It's been brought to my attention that we have some cross-collateralization issues, Mr. Gambini. Most of this coming from your recent, unfortunate separation." He frowned into the paperwork in front of him in one very neatly piled file about a half inch thick. It wasn't lost on me that "unfortunate" wouldn't be the proper word for this and could cut two ways. Did he mean unfortunate to be divorced, because I felt freed?

Or did he mean unfortunate because of what it had gutted from me and my businesses? I decided to ask.

"*Unfortunate* is a relative term, Mr. Cullen. I assure you, the best is yet to come. This was just a matter of pruning and tidying up." I tried to sound confident.

He wasn't buying it.

"I'd say it rather looked like having to give up one of your children, Mr. Gambini."

"Which, luckily, I don't have."

"Lucky for them as well, wouldn't you say?"

He'd just smacked me, and I was resisting the urge to see how flabby that belly of his actually was.

"I'd call it a haircut with a dull blade, Mr. Cullen. She was a bitch."

I decided to see what kind of metal he was made out of. His single eyebrow-raising gesture told me he didn't approve of my disparaging a woman. I normally didn't either, unless she deserved it. Rebecca certainly did.

"As you say, she could be, but she has a smart lawyer. I'd be careful who you go expounding your feelings to, Mr. Gambini."

He was a poser, and I salivated to dig my teeth into him.

"Is that a threat, Mr. Cullen? While we're being so helpful to one another, can I suggest you not say things like that to me? I could easily do business with someone else."

And then I felt brilliant as I saw the fear cross his face.

I stood up. "Don't answer that," I said to him, holding out my palm to his seated form. "I've just made my twentieth executive decision of the day. You can call Mr. Halliday in my accounting department and tell them you've gotten your bank fired."

He hadn't been prepared for this and started to stutter.

"With me, it only takes once. I don't give second chances, and I don't like threats. In case you didn't know, you just issued one."

I left.

It took me thirty seconds to catch a taxi. I'd just gotten seated when Frank dialed me.

"Not here—I'm in a cab," I barked.

"Marco, have him wait. Step outside so I can have a conversation with you." He sounded serious, with a dash of panic on the side.

"Just tell me, dammit."

As we sped toward the Towers I learned that there had been a call on one of my loans and cash was needed to keep the bank from foreclosing on me. My commercial dealings in Florida had been compromised by the recent filing of an injunction against the housing project on the beach for old frogs. Calling around, my

CFO had only located one bank willing to extend me a line of credit, based on my reputation and personal guarantee.

And I'd just pissed off that one bank willing to help me out.

"Just go back in there and tell him you made a mistake. It was a misunderstanding," Frank told me. I could tell he was pissed.

"Not on your life. Bankers get rich not by saying yes but by saying no as much as they can to cover all the bad yesses they make. I'm not going to give that sonofabitch the satisfaction."

"Marco, you have to face the facts."

"Fact is, Frank, I'm swimming with alligators, but I don't have to become a fuckin' yellow-finned tuna in the middle of the swamp."

"Yellow-finned tuna don't live in the swamp."

"My point exactly. I wouldn't make him that lucky and bestow on him such a miracle. Let him live on worms and rodents. There has to be another way."

"Marco, there is no other way."

"There always is another way!" I yelled. "Now don't call me back until you figure that out!"

I hung up. I felt the cabbie's eyes on me while I fussed. I wasn't proud of my anger or that I'd yelled at him and been abusive. I dialed him right back.

Before I could say anything, he blurted out, "I've

taken another job, and I'll be leaving on Monday. Maybe one of the sultan's daughters needs a good husband. You're that lucky, Marco, and way better looking than I am, so I think you could pull it off. But then, he'll own you. Have a nice life, Marco."

CHAPTER 8

Shannon

JARED WAS AS good as his word. He nailed the location of Rebecca's hotel in Clearwater by nine P.M. I called the hotel and got through to her right away, which surprised me.

"Your program director speaks highly of you, Shannon. He also stated you thought my interview this morning had been botched."

I was impressed Jared had the clout to be able to reach the ex-Mrs. Gambini, and even more by the fact that he told her about our conversation.

"I think she did a great disservice to your project, Mrs. Gambini."

"Oh please, I've been going by 'Hey Slut' now for the past year or more. You can call me Rebecca."

She did have balls the size of his. Okay, so much for one wrong mismatch. Maybe hers were bigger? I couldn't believe I was even thinking about his balls, and I certainly hoped she couldn't tell.

You really have the chops to make it if it doesn't go well?

Jared's question hung upside down in the bedroom of my belly, somewhere dropped around my ankles where my underpants went every time I thought about Marco.

"Thank you, Rebecca. In short, I think she dissed you."

"She totally dissed me, Shannon—or did I get that right?"

"It's Shannon, correct. I thought her comment about you taking over was disrespectful—almost as if she wished you'd fail."

"Well, I've dealt with little sluts before. Takes one to know one. If I didn't know it, I'd almost believe she was one of my husband's floozies."

"Oh, I'm so sorry. I didn't realize that—"

"Don't be. It's just my wild imagination. I can only imagine what he's doing and how many women are hitting on him now. He was a Navy SEAL, you know."

"Yes, I—" I had to stop myself or I'd send a vibe Rebecca's way that she was keen enough to pick up on. "I've read that was the inspiration for the project. A home for homeless SEALs. I didn't know there were any."

"A lot of people don't know how haunted they can

be. Some are driven. Some are haunted by their past." She sighed.

I surmised she was examining the grey clouds in the sky, detritus of the sunset nearly wiped away by now.

"You want to join me for a drink, or is it too late? You're a weather girl, right?"

"Actually, I'm a full-fledged reporter on a string to become a news reporter. They've just not discovered me yet."

That was the truest thing I'd said to her so far. I was jumping at the chance to join her but didn't want to appear too eager.

"Well, come on over. I'll grant that interview. Who knows? Maybe we can help each other out?"

"Thank you. Hope it isn't a big imposition."

"Not at all. I don't sleep well these nights. If I'm going to get drunk tonight, I might as well have company."

"You're on, then. So, you're at the Wyndham?"

"Yes, ma'am. Penthouse suite. Nice view of the Gulf, which you won't see much of at this hour of the night."

"I'll be over as fast as I can."

My fingers fumbled, my nerves buzzed throughout my body as if I was on a blind date with a Martian. This wasn't that kind of encounter of course, except for the fact that I had done all kinds of nasty things with her husband—rather, her *EX*-husband, the one she discarded and left up for grabs. And not only had I done those things, I wanted to do them over and over again.

I dropped my lipstick on the bathroom floor rug and had to toss it in the washer. I fluffed up my hair, pushed my boobs down in my minimizing bra and wore my sloggy black slacks under the oversized shirt that did nothing for my figure. One way to *not* win the trust and friendship of another woman is to do the "whose boobs are bigger, whose ass is tighter" thing, and reality didn't have anything to do with it. If she even *thought* I was prettier than she was, I'd be cooked liver without the onions.

I took a cab over since I knew I'd be drinking. He recognized me immediately.

"You smell as nice as you look Miss Marr." His wink was genuine and non-threatening.

"Thank you—" I checked the badge swinging from his rear-view mirror—"Carlos. Those modern flat screens have everything. I'll have to be more careful tomorrow tonight when I come on. Don't want to overpower the audience with too much perfume."

We both laughed.

The newly remodeled pink hotel was still pink in the late evening air, enhanced by rose-colored floods and a swarm of Flamingos who graced the lake and waterfall in front of the entrance. I was surprised they didn't put themselves to bed like chickens.

Inside the lobby, the night desk manager recognized and greeted me. He escorted me to the penthouse elevator, pushing the button and then stepping back. I fumbled for a couple of bills from my purse, but he smiled and shook his head.

"We're just happy you're here this evening, Miss Marr. Mrs. Gambini is expecting you."

About halfway up the floors I was struck with a sudden sense of impending danger. Just what in the hell had I gotten myself into, I wondered? I felt like a kite that had lost its tether, looking for a safe place to land (which was impossible for a kite).

Every story and scenario running through my brain was messed up. It was so bad that, if she hadn't greeted me in the hallway outside her suite, I might have pushed the button to go back down and caught a cab to run home. Maybe have a good cry on the beach. Find some of Judie's Scotch she left the last time she visited. Should I have called her first, just to make sure that if Rebecca murdered me when she found out what I'd done that someone could notify the police? Would I be afflicted by that talking disease that would make me blurt out something like, "He sucked me good, Rebecca. He screwed me so hard I couldn't sit down for days, and honey, I thought about him every time I crossed my legs and hoped his tongue was buried deep inside me."

Surely something nasty and venomous would come out of my mouth.

Nothing another nude encounter with him wouldn't fix. He could even be furious with me and want to beat me up, and I'd still sleep with him. Oh, God, I had it bad. And now I was about to jump into the cage of the tiger who, if she ever found out, would surely have me gangraped, tape it, and send it to him.

Or worse, have it played on one of those celebrity smut shows for everyone I ever cared about to see.

I bounced to attention, nearly biting my own tongue I was so hot for Marco, when she cooed at me, "Welcome, Shannon. I'm so glad you could make it!"

I walked behind her into her den, the torture chamber of my imagination. I was looking for the gangster guys who would be standing by with whips and chains and bungee cords. My life would come to a horrible screaming end. And Marco would never see me again as a person. I'd be a corpse he would identify by picture as, "Yes, I slept with her in Boston."

Such an ignoble way to go. She could even get away with it. Or, perhaps she'd shove me off the balcony. With my fear of heights, it would be the worst way for me to go, turning my lungs inside out with my screams, wetting and pooping in my pants as I made myself deaf just before I splattered my everything all over the concrete edges of that blue glorious pool I'd seen pictures of. I wouldn't even make it to the beach one more time. I'd be surrounded by lawn chairs, wet towels, and empty beer cans.

Rebecca had her hands on her hips and was smiling at me. Could she read my mind? This was worse than I imagined, and I could imagine a lot.

"I've seen your work, Shannon. You're very good with your arms, and you have graceful hands," she said as she winked. Her stare into my soul was way too long for comfort.

"Th-thank you." It was all I could think of.

Come. On. Shannon. You're. Not. Twelve.

It was like the day I saw a boy's penis for the first time because his friends at school had pantsed him. Even his butt cheeks blushed.

Really, Shannon? This the way you're going to start your big girl career?

Rebecca Gambini picked up a tumbler already prepared with a single ice cube, handing it to me with the brown liquid glistening inside the crystal, calling my name and laughing that I couldn't handle any hard liquor.

She shoved it into my chest, so I grabbed it.

"Come on, Shannon. Let's get shit-faced and tell

dirty stories," she said. I perked back to life when she loudly clinked my glass with hers like it was the clash of the titans.

Well, it was, sort of.

We both drank, and I was good at not spitting it back into her face, though I wanted to. For lots of reasons, I wanted to.

She added the warning I knew was coming. "And if you print a word of this, I'll sue your ass to the next century—I'll sue your parents, your siblings, and your children. Then I'll sleep with your husband and make him fall in love with me so I won't sue him."

She really said that. She. Did.

Rebecca was magnificent if she was anything. Except she was a total witch, not a bitch like I heard Marco said she was. She was red meat to a vegetarian. A cat with claw extensions to a tiny helpless mouse.

I was that mouse.

I knew I wouldn't survive the night.

CHAPTER 9

Marco

THERE WERE TIMES when it was necessary to keep my wits about me, and there were times when it was necessary to get drunk. I was even more dangerous when I got drunk, so I wanted to do it alone.

I ordered up some of Ollie's best Scotch and warded off his suggestion for the grape juice, orange liqueur, and cherries or whatever the hell it was that turned the drink into a Midnight in Manhattan. I was going to have the zombie apocalypse Manhattan with dried fruit and fish skeletons as stir sticks. I was having my own midnight in the garden of Marco Gambini's future, and it sucked big time. I didn't want anything diluting the drunk I was determined to accomplish tonight.

By drink number two, I was on my way.

Then I had a hankering for steak. And all of a sudden I wanted a new car, new clothes. I even wanted to set fire to my apartment at the Towers I hadn't even gotten properly dirty in yet. I shaved every day, trimmed my beard carefully with my expensive beard shaver, took a shower at least twice daily, carefully put away my dirty clothes, and laid out the clothes I was going to wear the next day.

I felt the need for the *Old* Marco Gambini to come out and play, that old crusty guy who didn't mind letting his beard grow wild and wore the same sweats and t-shirt for more than three days. I was hungry for lots of things, but steak would be first. Then I'd like to settle in and finish Ollie's bottle and watch porn. Maybe stumble into a bar at six in the morning or throw croissants at runners passing by while I sat outside on a park bench and tell them they were at least an hour late or ran too slow. I'd run if challenged. Even in my wingtips, I'd beat them. In my suit and tie, I'd beat them. I might hurdle park benches and sit with the bums and drink out of brown paper bags.

What good was it to be so razor-sharp ready for anything, prepared and regimented with my life if it was all turning to shit anyway?

It was *that* kind of a night, and it wouldn't be over until the sun came up and I could make the next day a shitty one too.

But first, that steak. Then I got a great idea. Fuck the bank who turned me down. Fuck the woman who screwed half of SEAL Team 3 in the old days, even though everyone told me she didn't. Fuck the flabby banker at East Coast who was probably screwing his secretary in the broom closet. Maybe I should go rescue her from that flabby fuck. I'd love to ring her chimes and bring her with me to Barbados where we'd lay naked on the beach and screw all day long.

But first I had to have steak. And my idea needed birthing. I dialed my Bentley dealer.

"Tony?"

"Holy crap, Marco, don't you know it's past midnight? Shit, it's one A.M."

"I know it. You have any Bentleys you haven't sold yet, a convertible?"

"Yeah," he yawned and mumbled into the phone.

"Can't hear you, Tony. I gotta have a Bentley."

"Sure. Sure, I got a red one, real pretty. Palomino interior, a real—"

"Wrap it up, put on your clothes and drive it to Boston."

"When? You mean now?"

"Yup. I'll give you an extra twenty-five thousand dollars if you get it here before the sun comes up."

"Oh God, Marco. Is this going to be one of those conversations you won't remember?"

"I'm writing it down. One. Red. Bentley. Convertible."

"Comes with a warning."

"What's that?"

"You gotta drive it sober, Marco. You'll love that thing but you'll wrap it around the first telephone pole you come across if you don't do it sober. And it's a babe magnet. You better hope not to go monogamous for at least two years. About the time it needs new tires, then you can trade it in, like all the others."

"Sold! I'll take it."

"Don't you want to know what it costs?"

"You think I'm worried you'll overcharge me and lose a good customer?"

"No, but don't you—"

"I'm using a credit card. Bring your machine when you come."

"No, I can't do that, Marco. You know it doesn't work like that. I'll take a check. Even an IOU will do, coming from you."

"Fine. Have it your way. Am I convincing you to sell me that red convertible?"

"Yes. You made the sale, Marco. I'll get it there as fast as is humanly possible. Will you be awake?"

"I will. I promise. If not, you can wake me."

"No harem, Marco. I'm not waking you up in a middle of little pink asses."

"Have I ever asked you to do that?"

"No, but just hearing your state of mind, I'm wondering…"

"Shut up. You're wasting time. You know where I live because you got me into this prison."

"So now it's my fault, is it?"

"Sort of."

"You're in a rather self-destructive mode. Are you sure you can afford this machine of mine?"

"I can. My credit is at least *that* good. Ask me to buy another 747 and the answer will be no."

"You need a woman, Marco, not a car."

"Nope. Already tried that."

"I mean a real woman, not a banshee."

I poured my fourth tumbler and remembered the smooth ass of the lady I pleasured a week ago. I wanted more of that, wanted to feel more of that. I wanted to stay in bed with her or in the back seat of the Bentley for a couple of lost days. I so needed just a couple of lost days…

And the lady lived in the Tampa area, which gave me another booze-filled brilliant idea. I was liking the images coming at me fast and furious…

"Are you still there, Marco?"

"Which would be faster, bringing the car to Tampa or to Boston?"

"Shit, Tampa's a thirteen-hour drive. I could make it to Boston in about six if I break the speed limit the whole way."

"Change of plans. Have the car delivered to the

Oceanis Resort in Belleair Beach. That's right outside of Tampa. Can you have it there tomorrow? I'll wire the funds in the morning."

"If you wake up, you mean."

"I'll be awake. I'm going to fly to Tampa tonight if I can."

"Why Tampa?"

"Something I forgot to do."

"Okay. I'll email all the information to Frank, as usual."

"Nope. We go direct on this one. Just have the car in Tampa tomorrow, earlier the better."

"Probably won't leave until the morning, but I think we can have it there tomorrow night before it's too late. What's so special about it?"

"I have plans for that back seat at sunset. So, make it before sunset."

"Then I'll have to start tonight. Fuck, Marco, are you sure you're okay?"

"Tony, I've never been worse, and I've never been better. I'm going to grab hold of something good, and if it isn't good, I'm going to hold it until it *is* good. But I don't have a lot of time. I have to be in D.C. by Tuesday."

"I hope you know what you're doing."

"One thing is for sure. It's either the dumbest thing in the world I could do or the best thing in the world.

I've already done some pretty good things, and I've just come off of doing a really dumb thing, so the odds are good I'll hit one of those extremes again. I feel it in my bones and some other places, too."

"Somehow I get the impression *there is* a woman involved."

"You could be correct."

"A reconciliation with Rebecca perhaps?"

"You just lost your twenty-five-thousand-dollar bonus, Tony."

"I don't want to take your money, Marco. I just want you to be safe."

"This is not only safe, it's a life-saver. It's going to change my life forever. Trust me."

"Well, if the president and the vice president and the secretary of state do, then I do as well. I'll get working on the papers now. And I better brew some coffee."

After he hung up I thought about the Tampa weather girl as I scanned the clouds lit up by the lights of the harbor district. I remembered she'd cried, for some strange reason, and it wasn't because I'd hurt her. It was because some kind of connection was made. I knew that connection was going to be just the lifeline I needed.

Maybe the thought of screwing—no, *making love*—in the back seat of that convertible with that beautiful, gentle, and intriguing woman was all a fantasy. But I willingly walked head-on into that fantasy, welcoming the images of her lips, her breasts, and the way it felt to make her shatter with her hips hugging mine and her arms holding me pressed against her. Her combination of softness, sweet female pheromones I hadn't experienced for years going back to before Rebecca, was something I'd missed and somehow overlooked.

I dared to peek under the carpet and examine that part of my life that belonged to Emily. I forced myself to feel the pain of her loss, staring right at the reality of how my life would have been different if she hadn't been killed in that accident. It was something I'd not had the courage to look for years. Somehow, Shannon brought back those days like a spirit from the past.

Maybe the old Marco hadn't been such a dumb fuck after all. Maybe that's where my mojo, my secret of success lay. It was a shame I'd laid it down with tuber roses and lilies at that little grave in Santa Rosa. Maybe, contrary to what I'd told myself these past fifteen years, that was the day all this craziness started and, maybe, just maybe it had nothing to do with Rebecca.

Well, I was going to find out. And if I didn't get all my answers, at least I'd have some new memories of sunsets and leather seats, soft arms and lips that craved to be pleasured. Maybe she was someone who needed me just as much as I needed her. In a few minutes I'd phone her, and make sure the welcome I'd felt was still present. I wanted her to anticipate my coming, to ready herself for someone to rock her world. It was better that she was fully ready to receive me rather than being surprised. Give her a chance to get out all the nice stuff and try to make an impression, because that's what I was going to do. I was going to woo her in a way she'd never been wooed before. She'd never forget this weekend.

Maybe we could need each other into oblivion, stop all the pain and hurt, and begin to heal in each other's arms.

There were crazier ways to find out, but I liked that it would start with an impulsive private flight to Tampa tonight, as soon as I got confirmation my pilot was ready, and I finished packing. It would continue with a fast drive to the gulf in an even faster red convertible. And maybe it would end with a sunset to all the darkness in my life, a bon voyage to all the misery and pain, and the start of a new day.

CHAPTER 10

Shannon

AS A DRINKING buddy, Rebecca made a fine one. I was actually having a great time, stumbling around, playing music, mostly oldies for her. Her favorites were all Em's favorite tunes too: Fleetwood Mac, Van Halen, even some Steely Dan thrown in. All these albums we found on her cell phone. We danced together like two long-lost friends. Except for her cutting wit and nasty language, it was almost like dancing with Em herself.

"Truth or Dare, Shannon!" Rebecca shouted, holding her glass high above her head. She turned down the music. "Best night *ever* when you were a teen?"

The oddness of the question made my insides flinch. I saw Marco, a much younger version of him, bending on his knee, presenting me with one of the flowers he'd plucked from the bouquet he'd laid at Em's coffin. His eyes were red, and his cheeks were streaked with shiny rivulets of tears. He couldn't talk, but I saw in his eyes the tremendous loss my sister caused him. How I wanted to ease that pain. He'd always been so kind to me, even defending me to Em sometimes. He was the bright spot in my Mother's Day whenever he showed up.

I was the invisible preteen.

"Remember her this way, kid," he'd said as he handed me the scented flower.

I would have preferred a hug or an itty bitty, teeny-weeny innocent peck on the cheek. He probably thought I was dumbstruck, my grief overwhelming me, which of course it did. But my small fingers shook as I took the flower, just to be in proximity to the man who had brought my big sister so much joy. I knew it would be the last time I'd see him, the last time our fingers would touch. I wanted to make it better by telling him how wonderful he made her feel, but I froze up. My knees locked. My insides shredded like an old curtain flapping in a glassless window frame.

"Yessss!" Rebecca hissed. "*That* one. What was *that* one about?"

I really had no idea why it would have been the best day of my life. It was certainly the most impactful. As the years went by, I saw that tiny flower not as a plant or once-living thing, but a torch given from one sister to another. Like the movie when the actress tells him to come back for her in time. Was he saying he'd see me later?

Of course not, and I was nearing the edge of sanity to think so. My head spun. I blamed it on the alcohol, which was also partially true.

"I think the Scotch has gotten to me. All that dancing. I'm dizzy. I need to sit down."

She was all over me like a mother, just like Em had, darn it. I couldn't get the thought of how similar and yet so dissimilar they were. I really wanted her to scrape her hands and arms from my body, but she clung to me because she was drunk too. She sat me down, carefully, on the couch, sat right next to me, and pushed my hair from my forehead.

"You're burning up, Shan."

Oh God! Not the name Em used to call me too!

I groaned and leaned into the couch back, which distanced my body somewhat from hers. She was on her feet, and nearly slipping and upturning the coffee table, she made her way to the fully stocked Penthouse kitchen, picked up a tea towel, and turned on the faucett so hard it splashed all over the counter, tile back, and her face and front. She screamed, then threw her head back and laughed. I recognized the reaction.

I resigned myself not to be surprised anymore. She acted so much like Em. Somewhere in my alcohol-sloshed brain, I understood that perhaps that's how he'd picked her. But the comparisons were driving me into a moroseness I didn't desire.

"I'm so sorry, pumpkin," she cooed, patting my face and forehead with the wet towel.

At last a name Em hadn't used!

"Thank you," I mumbled into the towel, helpless to do anything else and wishing I could get that day out of my head. But with Rebecca, I wouldn't be so lucky.

"I'm sorry I brought up something painful, Shannon. What was it? You can tell me."

"I-I really don't want to talk about it."

She lowered her chin, stuck out her lower lip, and gave me the puppy dog look I hated, which won me over all the time with Judie. "Please?"

Danger! Danger! Pitfall ahead!

Something inside me was trying to warn me off some course of action I'd regret forever. She laced her fingers through my hair, placing it neatly behind my shoulders. She took my hand in hers and squeezed.

"Talking about it might make it better."

"Believe me—" I started to say.

Her hand was up, taking no prisoners, shaking her head. Did she know she was really being cruel?

I pulled my paw from her grip and righted myself, cleared my throat, and asked for a glass of ice water.

"Gas or no gas?"

"What?"

"Sparkling or no?"

"Sparkling, if you have it."

"Lime, lemon, or orange flavored?"

All the choices right now I really didn't want to make.

"Lime."

"Good choice. My favorite too," she said breathlessly as she popped two bottle tops and returned with two tumblers full of ice to pour the sparkling water into. It was the needed delay I was seeking, but I knew I wouldn't escape.

Why *had* I thought of that moment when she asked about my best day ever as a teen? Again, I blamed it on the Scotch.

"Now. Spill the beans, Shannon. I promise nurse Rebecca will make it all better."

If she only knew.

"What you don't know is that I had an older sister. I'm not sure why, but I was reminded of the day of her funeral."

Rebecca clearly wasn't understanding my words. Her nose scrunched up. Her cheeks puckered to cover half of her eyes.

"I'm so sorry, pumpkin."

That name again...I was starting to hate it.

"But why? I mean, how come you thought about *that* day?"

I searched for something desperately to say. At last I came out with words I immediately regretted.

"You kind of remind me of her."

Rebecca moved away a couple of inches on the couch as if I was made of molten lava. Still watching me, she considered something. Then her shoulders dropped, and she sighed.

"I'm so sorry, Shannon. She sounds like a *wonderful person.*"

That comment sobered me up all of a sudden. Of all the selfish, wrong things to say to someone who was missing her sister, that was about one of the most heartless things she could have said. I was back on top, ready to complete the mission I'd set out to do. I'd have to be just as good a liar as she was. I could do that now.

"I think the reason I wanted to interview you partially was because of that. You do remind me of my sister. And, well, I thought I could do an interview that would do you justice, do her justice too, I guess." I shrugged. "In a way?" I raised my eyebrows into my hairline, opened my palms up on my lap, and waited for whatever was due me. I was such a sneak, such a bad person.

"I'm touched, Shannon," she said in her breathy, sexy tone, her expression brightening, almost becoming flirtatious. But I didn't get any sexual vibes, thank goodness. No, this woman was made of something else, and it was dark and deep. She was damaged goods, clear through. I reminded myself she was dangerous.

"I hope you didn't take offense, Rebecca."

"On the contrary. If I'd had a little sister, I could only hope that she would have been one half as sweet and cute as you, honey. But you've touched me. I want to help."

Uh-oh. She. Said. Help.

"Tell me about her."

"She was pretty." I looked up at Rebecca's eager face and the wild expression in her eyes and added, "Like you."

"Ah, that's nice of you to say. I'm not as pretty as I was once, but then, my next new boyfriend is going to be a plastic surgeon."

"New boyfriend?"

"My last boyfriend was an attorney who helped me with the divorce. I am eternally grateful, too. But my next one will be a gifted surgeon who loves to travel."

I tried to giggle, but it came out more like the lament of a pained cat. I coughed and took another long sip of mineral water.

"Go on. Tell me more about her. I'm fascinated."

"She was fun loving. She loved people and was always the life of the party."

"And you always felt mousy instead, am I right?"

That was not information she was entitled to. It

was only half of it, anyhow. I didn't feel mousy. I felt ignored because Em was such the favorite of my parents. I'd even told my mom one day when we argued years later that I wish I'd been the one killed so they could have continued living instead of the life they had with me. I'd gotten a slap for that comment and then a hug. Then we both burst into tears. My mother did the best she could but her heart was irreparably broken. Our mother-daughter bond was there because we had that pain in common.

"You're perceptive," I lied, trying to shed the sorrow that was being stubborn.

"How did she die?"

"It was an auto accident."

"Oh, so sad. You never got to say good-bye." Her lower lip was protruding, but it almost looked like she was mocking me. I began to see more difference between her and my sister. She didn't really have an ounce of compassion in her body.

"No. I didn't."

"Did she die right away, at the scene?"

The hairs at the back of my neck began to stand up. Did she have some morbid desire to dig into my pain, my past?

"Yes, we think so. My parents were devastated."

Rebecca stood and stared off into the dark bay, the lights of the pool and landscaped grounds reflecting back into her face, giving it a chilling light from beneath her chin like in some horror movie.

"What was her name?" she said absent-mindedly.

Did she suspect who I was? Even Marco didn't know who I was. I scrambled, but my tongue was thick, and my brain didn't function like it normally did.

"C-Connie," I blurted out. "Like Connie Stevens, the singer. Mom named her after her."

Rebecca nodded and opened the sliding glass door slowly, with cat-like movements.

"Come see the beautiful lights and the early morning air. It will be sunrise soon, Shannon."

"I-I'm afraid of heights, Rebecca. I'm so sorry, but I think maybe I should be getting home. I do go in early tomorrow. I have to set up my—"

Then I thought about the interview. I had neglected to ask her any questions. I had nothing to go work on. I could do background, but I'd already done some of that previously while researching Marco. I had to get something to show for the evening's meeting.

"Can I ask you some quick questions for the interview? I'd really rather talk about something else, if you don't mind. This was supposed to be all about you and the project, not me. And if I stand out there on the balcony, I'll unload all my dinner over the good people out there." I gave a sickly whinny.

She was the one being morose and very, very odd.

She looked down. "Lovers. There are only lovers out tonight, walking around the pathways, stealing kisses amongst the large palm fronds, watching the koi, and listening to the cicadas."

"Sounds beautiful, but I'm still staying put right here. If you don't want to do it tonight, how about you come into the station tomorrow? It's only a half-hour drive. Would you agree to that?"

"I can do that," she said as she closed the glass door, locked it, and floated over to sit at a forty-five-degree angle to me. She studied me. "Ask some of your questions now so I know the approach you'll take and I'll be prepared."

I fumbled for my cell phone, where I'd stored several questions. There was a call I'd missed from Boston, since I'd turned off my ringer. I scrolled to my notepad.

"Um, we already know you like to dance and sing. Tell me about the project and why this is so important to you?"

"Because Navy SEALs deserve a home. They fight. They leave their whole lives out there on the battlefield. Sometimes, they come back empty. They lose their families often, everyone but their brothers. So many of them die lonely, misunderstood, and without the support of those who loved them or could help them. They prefer the company of their teammates. And it's hard for a family to understand how lonely they are."

"That's so wonderful that you do. Having been through it, of course," I added, thinking it was a safe comment.

But her eyes morphed into slits. "You don't know anything about my relationship. It was completely different. But that's another interview for another day."

"Of course." I nearly dropped my phone, scrambled for my notes and read off another question. "So tell me how the idea came to you, and how do you imagine it going forward?"

"It didn't come to me. It was Marco—that's my husband—my ex-husband, I should say—it was Marco's idea from the get-go. I actually fought him on it. But after I saw what a mess he was making of his businesses, I decided to resurrect his mission, since he didn't have the money or the time."

"How good of you." I gulped down more water, taking some of my bile with it.

"I admit, at first I did it to make him mad, but you won't put that in the interview, will you?"

"Of course not."

"That's a good girl," she said with a strong dose of condescension. I was starting to hate her now. Again, I thought it might be the alcohol talking/feeling/confusing me.

She began again. "I thought it might be a good idea

to hang around some of those hunky silver foxes. SEALs are an odd lot. Strong yet so weak in the relationship cajones, if you know what I mean. They fall for women easily and then don't know what to do with them once they've gotten them. They certainly know how to use their equipment—"

I blushed. She noticed.

"Shannon, you're holding out on me..." She was smiling, but I still felt under her thumb.

"Your comment, well, I was thinking about—what I'd heard—about SEALs. I mean, they're supposed to be great lovers, and all." I quickly added, "*Not* speaking from experience, of course."

She chuckled. "My husband was an expert at everything. He qualified expert in his diving, firearms, demolition, languages. He was the fastest runner on his team, even the day he disengaged. And he could make me wet just by looking at me. He could make me wet with his little finger, with his tongue..."

I stepped on my own tongue and quickly closed my mouth. My blush was obvious.

"It turns you on just to hear me talk about it, doesn't it, Shannon?"

I knew I had to be very careful. While I was foggy-brained from the alcohol, Rebecca's wits were becoming sharper, more honed. I realized that it was where she lived as a woman. She was a competitor, a pure driver who liked to be in control even when she was drunk. I could see that competing against Marco would make her feel stronger, not weaker. She lived for it, in fact. Em was competitive in that she never gave up, especially hope.

"Well, I've never had this kind of conversation, and this certainly won't go into the interview."

"Oh, I know it won't. Because it will reflect badly on you. But come to the interview tomorrow with those thoughts in mind, and then we'll have a real girl chat, on camera. Let's not tape it. Let's go live and bare."

I was dumfounded, sure my program manager would never approve of this. I was thinking about how I was going to tell him. It was on impulse that I answered her, with more guts than brains, as if someone else were talking through me. "Okay, Rebecca, let's do it. Don't know if it will get approved, but I'll try to make that happen. Let's fly off into the history books—together, like real sisters."

She threw her head back and laughed so hard I thought she and the chair would flip over backwards.

Then my phone rang. I really should have checked who had called me. I knew better. But I didn't. I was so worried about what I was going to do tomorrow and how I'd pull this off without ruining the station's or my reputation, it didn't occur to me that things were about to heat up even hotter.

"Hello, Shannon."

It. Was. Marco. The sound of his sexy voice slithered down my spine and ignited my sweet spot. I felt the pulsing wetness between my legs.

"Oh, hello." I sounded and felt like I was twelve, my voice cracking. "It-it's kinda late. Could I call you back?" I whispered.

"Are you with someone I have to come over and strangle? Want me to?"

"Well, you're not here—I'm in Clearwater."

"I'm getting ready to fly to Tampa as we speak. I thought perhaps we could have breakfast when I arrive, and then I could book you for dinner at sunset, if you'd be agreeable."

I was so agreeable I was nearly wetting my pants. And then I saw the smirk of the woman across the coffee table from me. She had a Cheshire cat grin.

"That would be nice. But can I call you back?"

"You *are* with someone."

"It's not what you think, M—Mike."

"Mike? You're a nasty little girl, Shannon. I want to know more. I want to hear you whisper it to me when I pump you full of everything I've got."

Oh dear God! My face, my chest, my boobs were fiery red, engorged and tingling. My pounding heart was making it difficult to breathe. And my panties were so wet I could even smell them.

Rebecca was trying to listen, her eyebrows raised. I made sure to press the phone to my ear and wished I'd brought my earpiece.

"Listen, call me when you get here, please" I tried not to make it sound like a beg. "I'm with a girlfriend and your comments, well, they're embarrassing me." I gave a wide-eyed sweet smile to his ex, and that made everything worse.

"But are you looking forward to my visit? Just tell me because I won't come if you have to rearrange your whole schedule..."

Marco, you could rearrange my whole life! My brain was shouting, my inner angel was beating up the lonely witch inside me.

"Of course I am. Very much so. A pleasant surprise. Tomorrow, then?"

"I can't wait."

"Neither can I," I said, staring right into the eyes of his ex-wife.

I DON'T REMEMBER how I got home, but I did. I don't know how she believed that my boyfriend was coming to Tampa for a surprise visit. If she only knew.

I took a shower, washing my hair so I didn't smell anything like Rebecca or her motel room. I laid out something I hoped I'd look spectacular in and tried to sleep the two or three hours until morning.

But it was impossible. My body needed rest, but it was all fired up, wide awake and unrelenting. My eyes were going to look so red. My heart was pounding in my chest so loud I felt like I was shaking the windows. And I had to do that interview with Rebecca at ten A.M. Right after my breakfast with Marco. And if he got here late, well, I'd have to cancel it.

I toyed with the idea of having someone else do the interview and thought, as I walked on the beach at sunrise, that that would save my bacon. There was only so much a girl could do. He was hot on my trail. He wanted me. There was no question I'd be sleeping with him and partaking of that elixir he so deliciously gave out. I was helpless, talking to him while she was watching. It was like the question she asked me, "What was the best day ever…" Well this was the worst and the best day ever.

And I knew it would get worse before it would get better. I hadn't been wrong about his attraction for me. It *was* mutual, after all, not some figment of my imagination.

As I walked the beach in my bare feet, I clutched the phone in my right hand, waiting for the call that would change my life forever.

If I didn't screw the whole thing up.

Now I really had to start going back to church.

CHAPTER 11

Marco

I WAS CUTTING it close to get to Tampa by breakfast, since the flight itself would take three-plus hours. My pilot was ready, but the jet wasn't quite. That gave me time to shower and shave again, finish packing and take a car to the airport. We were wheels up less than fifteen minutes after I arrived.

The attendant my pilot brought along mixed me a mimosa and handed me an assortment of vitamins and lots of Vitamin B, probably understanding the condition I'd been in when I booked the flight. I passed on any further alcohol, took my pills, and promptly fell asleep.

I landed just as it turned seven A.M. The bright sun was scalding my pupils. It had been a few very grey days in Boston, with light drizzle occasionally, so coming into the moist warmth of Florida's Gulf Coast was very welcome indeed, but an adjustment, nonetheless.

I tried to remember the conversation I'd had with Shannon just a few hours ago, but I did remember she agreed to meet me for breakfast and dinner later on, and she wanted me to call when I landed. I did so now.

"I'm in Tampa. Just landed."

She hesitated, sounding a little nervous. Well, I was a little nervous too. It felt like prom night all of a sudden.

"I'm sorry about last night. I had a few too many, and..." she began.

"You too? I hope you didn't have the kind of day I had."

"I'm not sure you could have. It wasn't one of my finer moments. I don't think you'd believe me if I told you."

"All forgiven. I'm here now. I can't remember what I said last night, but I believe I did invite you to breakfast and you agreed. And dinner too, is that right?"

"Yes." She giggled. "That part I remember."

"I hope I wasn't too—well, I was pretty wasted."

"So you want to reconsider the whole thing then?" she said sharply.

"Not at all. As a matter of fact I was looking forward to it, dreaming about it."

She didn't say a thing, and I got worried.

"Marco, I have an appointment at the office at ten

this morning, unless I can get out of it, and I'm going to try but can't reach anyone there. So if you're not up to it, we can skip breakfast. What I'm trying to say is that it wouldn't be a problem."

"Are you telling me you'd just rather meet me in my motel room?" Before she could answer I abruptly cut in. "I'm sorry. That wasn't very respectful of me. You seem to bring out both the best and the worst in me, Shannon. I promise to be on my best behavior."

I began to exit the plane as she replied.

Her raspy voice instantly got me even harder. "I don't mind your bad behavior. Was sort of looking forward to it, but I was just saying that I don't mind if we skip breakfast and just have dinner, if you're too busy."

I decided to tell her the truth. "I came here to see *you*. This is not a business trip for me."

"But your project—?"

"Will still be there after breakfast and probably after dinner as well. I want to see you." I hoped I didn't sound too desperate, but I was beginning to feel some hesitation on her part. I meant it when I told Tony that I was going to hang on until she'd let me rock her world, and I meant every word of it.

"I want to see you too."

It was music to my ears.

"Where should I meet you?"

"I could fix some eggs if you're not too picky, Marco."

"Your place. You're inviting me to your place?"

"It's not fancy. Just a little bungalow at the beach about a half mile from your project."

"Ah, so you've checked up on me?"

"Of course I have. You wouldn't expect anything less, right?"

"I'm flattered."

"So how do we do this, Marco? You tell me."

"Text me your address and I'll be over there in about a half hour, depending on traffic."

"It's Saturday. No traffic. I'll see you then."

My driver took me to a local florist shop inside one of the supermarkets, the only place open, and I selected a bright bouquet of flowers, which I thought safer than roses. I'd bring her roses at dinner, but for this morning these would have to do. The clerk wrapped them in green tissue and placed a pink bow on them.

She lived off the main Gulf Blvd. on a side street that served houses that fronted the beach itself at Indian Rocks. Her house was one of the more modest structures, but it was surrounded by McMansions.

I heard music coming from her frosted glass front door. I knocked and found her fresh face even more beautiful than I'd remembered, and I'd remembered a lot. I extended the flowers to her, but before she could take them, I slipped my arm around her waist and pulled her into me. She arched backwards, slid her arms up over my shoulders, and pulled my head down to hers where we ignited the flame of our past encounter. The long lingering kiss could have easily lead to something more, right there in the doorway to her little house, in front of the eyes of my driver. It was the welcome I had hoped I'd receive.

I turned my head and nodded, indicating he could go, and he did so after giving me a salute.

She welcomed me into her living room and this time, took the flowers from me, burying her nose in them.

I was fascinated with her collection of artwork. She had a variety of acrylic paintings of some of the beach bungalows I'd seen previously on my visits here. There were a few watercolors and several beach plaques with beachy sayings on them. Perhaps she made some of these, but they were locally produced.

Her small living room was dwarfed by the enormous butter yellow leather couch that had been well worn and sun-bleached, as it faced the ocean and beach beyond behind a huge glass window. Something about the whole scene was oddly familiar to me. It felt very safe.

I turned to face her, and she erupted.

"Oh my gosh, I'd better get these in some water."

She dashed off into her bedroom, closing the door behind her. A few seconds later, she came out.

"Wrong room," she said as she blushed and headed for the kitchen. "Would you like coffee?"

"I'd love some."

She arranged the flowers and then poured me coffee. "Cream?"

"Of course."

"There you go."

I couldn't choose between the steaming mug of delicious-smelling coffee and the vision in front of me. I set it down, and held my arms out wide.

"Come here, Shannon. I don't want you to be nervous with me. You know by now I'm a man who knows what he likes, and I want more of what we had. There was something…"

She held her fingers over my lips and kissed me.

My hands moved over her ass, then up under her shirt, seeking her nipples as we kissed. Her fingers unbuttoned my shirt, and soon her lips were tasting my wartime badges, the ink I had placed on my body to remember everything, the good and the bad of it all.

She undid my fly, and I hissed, inhaling as her fingers found me.

We separated, breathing hard, looking into each other's eyes, and then she took my hand and led me to the bedroom.

I sat down, removing my shoes and socks while I watched her undress in front of me. She laid my shirt on a side chair, folded, and placed my jeans underneath. I slipped off my briefs, revealing the hard-on I'd been sporting for several hours now.

She was still in her bra and panties as she took a condom from her nightstand, kneeled in front of me and pressed it over my shaft. She rubbed my balls and ran her forefinger up the underside over the condom.

I released her bra and slipped her panties down to her ankles and then parted her knees. I watched her eyes as I fingered her carefully, feeling how ready she was and watching her arousal fuel my own. Then I crawled back up onto the bed, leaning against the cloth headboard, waiting for her to come to me.

Her knees slid over my hips to straddle my lap, and I slid inside her slowly at first, then deeper, and at last fully seated as she writhed above me. I wanted to feel every ripple, every moan coming from her body. Her soft mouth and tongue tempted me to go deep, so after several minutes of soft sex play, I flipped her onto her stomach, held her belly up with one hand, and smoothed over her butt cheeks with the other as I took her from behind. Hard. Her body resisted me at first, and I worried she was so tight the condom would break as I pumped her furiously.

It all changed when her orgasm started. Her spasms

began, slamming against me, pulling me deeper inside her channel. I was filled with lust at her moaning and loss of control. I pulled out to taste her. She screamed in frustration, but I wouldn't relent. My tongue was already lapping her juices. I spread her knees wider to gain more access, and she tried to reach back to touch the top of my head. She gripped her own buttocks, spreading them wider still for me, dug her knees into the bed, and pressed herself up into my face. I played with her, lapping and sucking until she begged me to go deep again.

Slipping my thighs between hers, I gently lifted her by the waist, seating her on my lap as I buried my cock deep to the hilt. She gasped as I held her in place. It felt so perfect, so good to pleasure her and feel the turmoil going on inside her.

She leaned back against me, and we tried to kiss. I bit her earlobe, and whispered, "I love fucking you. Your sweet body was made for me. I should never have let you go that morning. What. Was. I. Thinking?" I said as I pumped to her screams.

Her fingers laced with mine as I pinched her nipples, and made her squeal.

"Come for me, Shannon. Let me feel it while I fill you."

She groaned, ground down on my lap as I pushed up and pressed against her sweet spot, ardently knocking on the door of her womanhood as my shaft swelled against her pulsing muscles. I burst up inside her as she came totally apart.

I held her tight so she wouldn't careen over the side of the bed, she was so limp. She clung to me like a rag doll. I kissed the sides of her neck, probed and pressed her little hot nub with my forefinger, making her bounce against me as I completed my mission. I pulled her hair up from her neck and kissed her sweaty skin until I was nearly spent.

We crashed into the bed, a tangle of sheets, legs, and arms, her orgasm coaxing and prolonging mine until we were both completely wrung out.

She clutched my hand in hers, drew it to her chest, curled like she'd done before at the Towers, and fell asleep tucked into my arms.

This time, she didn't cry.

CHAPTER 12

Shannon

WE MUST HAVE slept for an hour or more. My cell phone rang, but there wasn't any possibility I'd be able to extricate myself from Marco's arms and legs to answer it in time. His hand lightly rubbed my shoulder as I looked up and into his face and gave him a kiss.

"So much for breakfast," I yawned. "But I might have time to whip something together," I whispered.

"If you do it naked and I can watch."

"I think I can arrange that." I started to move, sliding off the bed, but he grabbed me and had me pressed against his chest again.

"I changed my mind. I'll have you for breakfast."

"But I have an appointment at the office."

"Cancel it."

I knew I had to tell him. Now was as good a time as ever, or he'd never understand why I had to rush off. He'd go digging, and I didn't want him showing up at the station while in the middle of the interview. I searched his face just in case it was the last time I'd see how lovingly he smiled at me. I sat up, looking down on him as he settled his arms beneath his head on the pillow.

"What's up, Shannon?"

"I have to tell you something. You might not like it."

"Oh? I doubt you could ever say or do anything I wouldn't like. So why do you think that?"

"Trust me. I've gotten to know a little about you."

He remained relaxed on the outside, but I could sense he was very alert on the inside. He drew the back of his hand across my cheek and brushed against my lips as I kissed his lingering fingers. "Yes you have. And I believe it goes both ways."

He waited.

"I have taken on an interview this morning. It was arranged before I knew you were coming, or I certainly wouldn't have done it. But it's a human-interest story."

In my silence, he whispered, "What, Shannon?"

"It's a story on your housing project for Navy SEALs. And I'm interviewing Rebecca today at ten. That's who I'm meeting."

At first he didn't believe me. Then his eyes got dangerous and he began to breathe deeply. He stared at the ceiling and stopped touching me. I knew telling him was the right thing to do because he'd find out anyway. But I so regretted having to tell him at that moment. Out of the side of my vision I could see he'd focused on me again with something deep and penetrating. I slowly returned his gaze and started to explain further. I was even prepared to give an apology, but he put a finger to my lips.

"Does she know?" he asked.

"Does she know what, Marco?"

"About this. Us. Boston." His voice was a little louder, anxious and scratchy.

"No. Never in a million years."

His eyes didn't wander from mine. I knew he was serious. "I want you to tell her after the interview. Tell her you love sucking my cock. Tell her we're gonna screw all day and all night."

While I was mildly pleased he didn't toss me from the bed and leave, I could see that I had hurt him, and he was reacting like I knew he would. A wounded bear. As he began to say something in anger, it was my turn to stop him with my fingers to his lips.

"No, Marco. She has nothing to do with us. Nothing about us has anything to do with her, unless you bring her in."

His eyes sparkled, new light brightening the darkness at the centers. He cocked his head to the side to listen.

"I'm going to just go in and do my job. She'll find out or not, but not from me and not this morning before or during the interview. You have my permission to tell her if you want, because that's not my call. It's yours."

"Really? You'd let me do that?"

I couldn't tell if he was being sarcastic because his mood was still stormy, but I relied on the color in his eyes and those tiny smile lines at the sides of his lips. And his voice. He was soft, if not raspy. He was patient, staging himself in case he had to control an outburst. I could tell all this just because I'd seen it years ago when he argued with Em about getting married. He'd held her off, and although she cried into his arms, he promised to return to her after that first deployment. And he did.

She was the one who didn't return. They never had counted on that.

"Why spoil our chances with each other, Marco? This is all new, exciting, and exactly what I want. Don't let her spoil it, like she's spoiling the rest of your life. Don't give her that much power."

He reached out to touch my arm, and then changed his mind and covered his eyes with his forearm. I wasn't going to let him know his emotions were showing no matter how much he tried to hide them up. That was part of the Marco I wanted to be with.

"So don't bring that woman into our bedroom," I said as I peeled his arm from his face, took his hand in mine and kissed his palm. He watched. Then his powerful fingers slid up my neck, into my hair, where he took fistfuls and pulled me down so he could ravage me with kisses.

"I need to fuck you, Shannon. Hard," he whispered in my ear, flipping my body over onto my back.

"Oh God, yes!" I said, relieved, my arms pulling him down on top of me. It was the only answer I was capable of giving him. My body wasn't nearly enough, but I didn't mind sharing my complete surrender to him. He took a chance on me, and I wanted him to feel like he could take me any time.

I was his vessel. I didn't stop him to put on a condom he never asked for because it didn't matter what the outcome was. Judie would tan my hide if she ever found out how risky it was, but I just didn't care how un-modern and stupid I was being. There were some things more important than being appropriate.

My tears were hot but silent as he thrust into me and wildly pumped. He slipped his arms beneath me and pulled my shoulders down so we could mate as tight as possible, picking up the intensity. I thought the bed would rock off the frame, or we'd break it. I felt the bulging muscles in his back as he worked feverishly to his peak.

"Can you come for me?" he whispered in my ear.

I didn't answer him. His pause was brief. Then he resumed his earlier frenzy. At last I felt him pulsing inside me, and then he started to pull out. I held his buttocks with both hands, pressing him deeper and telling him not to stop. I accepted every drop unconditionally.

Afterward, he collapsed onto my chest, and we caught our breaths together. He finally looked up at me and brushed my eyebrows with his thumb, nibbling on my lips. "You should have stopped me, Shannon."

I shook my head, brave to let him see my tears. "I wanted it too, just this way. Because what I think I have here with you is real, and I've thought a lot about it. Marco, for however long it lasts, we belong together right now. Here. I'm not going to let her take any of that away. It's just us."

He turned his head as if carefully considering my words. Heck, I didn't even believe it myself. Evaluation and calculation were ruminating inside his brain. I knew he was trying to figure out if he could trust what I said.

He frowned. "It's still not how I want to treat you. You deserve more."

"I would have stopped you, and you would have honored my request. For me, Marco, you were never out of control, and I trust you. As crazy as it feels, I do trust you."

I was looking for another word that wasn't appropriate, and I stuck to my guns and reverted to the safe Shannon who wasn't going to press him, even though I was his completely.

Then he asked me, "How did all this come about?" He was still nibbling on my neck, putting his tongue in my ear, biting my earlobe, making me ticklish. I loved the intimacy between us, as if we'd been lovers for decades.

"I saw her interviewed on another program yesterday. I had no idea you were going to call, to come here. I asked my program manager if I could also do an interview because I did want to do one on your project anyway. And I guess I was also a little bit curious about her."

"Did you satisfy your curiosity?" he whispered.

"I have no right to say it, but she's not good for you."

He stared back down at me without moving a muscle.

He was beginning to make me nervous, so I continued explaining, hoping he was as calm about it as he seemed.

"But I did it so I could begin to do a piece on your work, this project. Did I hope that somehow it would lead to you? I'd have to answer that question with a yes.

But if I'd have known about you coming here, that you did want to see me again, I never would have set this up. And now I'm very sorry. But trust me, Marco. She is not part of our relationship. She belonged to the man you no longer are. I have this one," I said as I pressed my hand against the tat of the sun on his chest over his heart. "For however long you'll grant me access, I want this. I want us."

He watched me and, after a brief few seconds, placed his hand over mine.

"You be careful, Shannon. She's dangerous."

"Yes, I already know that."

He angled his head. "So, you've met her already?"

I didn't want to answer.

"She was the person you were with last night when I called?"

I wasn't proud of my answer but this wasn't the time to start lying to him. "Unfortunately, yes."

"And you don't think she knows?" His voice was beginning to raise. "If she could hear my voice—"

"No, Marco. She didn't. It was one of the most awkward moments of my entire life. I promise you I kept that phone tight to my ear."

"Because she'll hurt you if she can. You know that, right?"

I nodded.

"She knows I'm out to get her. She'll hurt you to get

to me, Shannon."

"I'm not a part of that war, and like I said, she has no standing, no place in this relationship. Tell me you agree and understand that. I need to hear it. Or, am I wasting my time?"

It was one of the hardest things I'd ever had to ask.

"What do you think?"

I couldn't tell him that I'd known him for over fifteen years, followed his career and how he lived because I'd studied it. And I knew he wouldn't just use me and walk away, but he didn't know that. I knew I'd have to do the reveal about Em some day and probably soon before we got too involved, but today wasn't that day. But if we became a couple, a real couple, it would have to be done. Right now, I wasn't sure what we were except a bright new beginning of something magic.

"I'm right where I want to be, Marco. I think you feel the same."

"I want this too," he whispered. "No more secrets, Shannon, okay?"

He must have felt my body flinch, but I softened it with a lazy smile. God, I was being such a good actress, or I hoped I was anyway. Because I really did want this to work, and I prayed that he'd forgive me somehow when it came to Em.

His face broke into a smile. "I guess you like to live a little on the dangerous side of life, maybe a little like me, then. You're an adrenaline junkie too. Not a drama queen. Is that what you're saying?"

"I'm responsible for all this, yes. But did I plan it that way? Hell no. I'm not going to try to cover up what I've done. I can't do that to you, Marco. If you can't trust me, what do we have?"

"It still would have been worth it, honey," he said, lovingly adjusting my hair over my shoulder so he could look at my breasts again. I was relieved when he kissed my nipples one by one, and added, "But I like the idea of a sunset dinner somewhere special and, who knows? Maybe there will be more."

"I want more, Marco."

"Don't I scare you? You should be scared, you know?"

Not being able to be with him was the scary part. Maybe I did like to live dangerously because if I ever had to get over him, I knew I never could.

"I want the way I feel when I'm with you. I want the man I think I'm beginning to know. That man, who's gentle, who protects and keeps me safe. I'll do battle with anyone because my biggest fear is losing this."

That got him chuckling. "I'm supposed to be thinking about a big meeting I have in D.C, on Tuesday and a trip I have to take halfway around the world. Also, a job I will probably have to oversee in Africa. I have to look for a new CFO. And I have to deal with a loan called against my assets and show up in court to produce documents."

His hand fished down under the covers until he touched my wet, throbbing sex. Then, as he delicately fingered my opening and pressed a thumb into my clit, he spoke very seriously, directly to my face.

"But, all I can think about is a weather girl in Tampa with the softest skin and the sweetest kisses. I can't stop fucking her in my dreams, in my bed, in your bed. Anywhere. I can't stop, Shannon. I don't want to lose this, either."

My tears flowed. I just couldn't help them. Part of it was relief, but part of it was knowing that the other secret I'd been holding onto might be the end of us. I knew my life would be a lot easier, but duller, if I'd never gone to Boston, met him, and fell in love that first time.

There was that word I couldn't speak of.

But it was too late for that. I was in deep. And there was a world war ahead for me to win first.

CHAPTER 13

Marco

IT WAS HARD to let her go. We nearly didn't make it out of the shower. I quickly dressed, and she dropped me off at the Oceanis, which was on her way to the radio station.

"Come check out the room I've got, Shannon," I begged, knowing it would do no good.

"No, Marco," she said, shedding my hand as I tried to pull her inside the lobby.

I grabbed my leather bag, gave her one more kiss, and waved as she drove away.

"Checking in, sir?" the bellman asked.

I was directed to the front desk.

After signing the registration card, I was handed a small sheaf of papers, messages from the office in D.C., the old office in Manhattan, and from the Towers in Boston. I knew, of the three, the one from the Towers would be the most innocuous so dialed them on my way to the elevator.

Jerrold Hoffstedler from the accounting office sounded like he was still in high school, complete with the croak in his voice that made me think it had just changed. His nasal tone was a little off-putting. Perhaps he had a sinus infection.

"We're having trouble processing the balance of your lease deposit, Mr. Gambini. It seems the bank says you're overdrawn."

"That can't be. I have millions. Used to have billions. I've not been overdrawn for nearly twenty years."

"I know it's probably some glitch in your accounting system. You were approved without any problem, which means they checked your assets. These things happen all the time when we have guests relocating from other metropolitan areas. I once had a Saudi prince who bounced a three-hundred-thousand-dollar check to us. He was quite embarrassed."

"I should hope so."

"I'm sure it's a condition of moving and something just didn't get flagged properly. If you could call us back tomorrow or Tuesday, there won't be any further action needing to be taken."

I was hoping that my CFO wasn't giving me a good-bye headache. He left because he was scared he'd not have a job if he didn't. But I doubted he'd do anything vindictive. In fact, I was sure of it.

But Rebecca, on the other hand, was another story entirely.

The suite I'd hired was spectacular. The views spanned nearly fifty miles of white sand beach coastline. I felt like the King of Atlantis, above the gulf, even above the gulls and pelicans flying through the blue sky containing billowy clouds the largest I'd ever seen. It would be a spectacular sunset. I threw my leather bag on the bed, and began to plan out what I was going to order for dinner.

The concierge helped me coordinate the delicacies I was seeking. She reminded me that there were monogrammed towels, robes, and blankets in the bedroom closet and let me know if I needed any more, she'd send them right up. I felt confident handing over all those details, including the most fragrant long-stemmed red roses she could find.

"Is this a marriage proposal, Mr. Gambini?"

"No. Just someone very special. And if tonight goes well, then anything is possible."

"Oh I'm so excited to help you with this. Clients like you are why I have this job. I'll put on my thinking cap and call you back with some ideas after I've made some calls. You shouldn't worry about a thing."

I laughed. If only.

It was out of the question I would call the East Coast Bank & Trust, in either Manhattan or Boston, but I had to get the loan covered or this alligator would have a bunch of babies. And then I'd be asking for a job at the front desk, or selling Bentleys with Tony.

And that reminded me! I had a Bentley coming soon. I called the pretty concierge and told her to let me know when it arrived and to have several blankets placed into the trunk and figure out how I could keep a bottle of champagne chilled when I drove the beast. She squealed and promised it was a task she'd lovingly carry out.

But it was time to face my financial woes. I'd let the bank stew long enough. I believed there was another way to handle my predicament and remembered Frank's comment. I didn't have the answer yet, though.

My attorney was the call from D.C. and I called him next.

"Marco, not getting much cooperation from Frank. Is he on an extended vacation? Seems like he took his whole office staff with him."

Great. So much for simply fading into the woodwork.

"He's on a temporary assignment," I lied. "What can I help you with?"

"I'm being pressured for financials for the Trident Towers. You remember, we had that subpoena we had to produce documents? I've asked three times for a Performa P&L from his office and I get crickets. You wouldn't have that kind of information with you, I take it?"

"You know I don't."

"Well, they shut down the office in Belleair because there was a shortfall for payroll. Looks really bad when that happens. I thought you were tending to that with the transfers so this didn't have to happen. It's bad press."

"Have Celia in the HR department issue a memo about bonuses coming before Halloween, just in time for the holidays. An extra bonus for all their hard work and to thank them for their patience. And get them back to work."

"Yes, yes, we can do that, but we don't want to run afoul with Florida or Federal employment law. They'll have to be paid first."

"That's going to be my next call. Don't worry about it. All but on its way."

"Never mind the damage control. What I want to know is how did it happen?"

"I had a loan called."

"How much are we talking?"

"Ninety million."

His whistle was long and loud. "Are we solvent?"

"Of course we are, Bob. I could sell a couple of airplanes and raise the cash, given enough time."

"So where's the hole in the piggybank?"

"Guess. Where is it always? She got to somebody, and it started a domino effect."

Rebecca had intimidated the staff at the interior design group's office so much that one time she had overspent funds to redecorate our new build-out in Manhattan, a state-of-the-art center with an interactive display showing all the hot spots in the world today, and how one thing always leads to another. It was a brilliant idea, showing how something that happens in Africa could affect the price of water in the San Joaquin Valley for pear and prune farmers. Nothing was ever as simple as it was laid out in the large metropolitan newspapers. Stuff was always brewing just below the surface—stuff the general public and half our government didn't know about. But I did. I tracked these every day.

But even though it was a brilliant success and widely acclaimed as a masterpiece lobby, she spent twice as much as she was authorized. She had them all shaking in their boots, intimidated to the point of trying to hide that big goose egg under fear of being fired, until one of the junior clerks manned up and came to me, spilling the beans. He was the only one in that design department to keep his job.

That was the beginning of my seeing what she was doing. It was like Chinese torture—holding my eyes open with toothpicks. We had the longest and loudest argument of our marriage. In the process, she destroyed a whole package of carefully wrapped paintings I'd just purchased to add to my extensive collection. I retaliated by grabbing her box of jewelry and throwing it off the balcony where it fell into the pool and marble surround at the Ritz in Paris, the place we were staying.

She became caustic and bitter, and we never made up. We fucked like dogs in heat, occasionally and rarely, but we never made up.

We never would.

Her new tactic of tying up my assets and putting holds on funds already approved for different projects, which, at the front end anyway, usually meant paying the visionaries to get the ball rolling on a new project, was what she had done since the divorce. I couldn't figure out why she still would have such a hard-on for me. She got nearly everything she'd wanted in the settlement.

But there was one thing she didn't like hearing, and my attorney rammed it hard into her and was unrelenting. She had the special clause he'd designed stricken from the settlement agreement. The language required that she distance herself from me, my companies, and my employees for the rest of her natural life. If there ever was any doubt, I was severing all ties to her, that clause was living proof I was as serious as a heart attack. She was to go away and never grace my doorway again. I'd paid a lot of money to make sure she would do that.

It took months, and even though she refused to sign it, we still left it in the agreement because I wanted it there, lined it out in red, and both of us eventually initialed it so we could be done.

But that's exactly what she was refusing to do. She was determined to continue to ruin me further by these antics and little surprises I had to juggle to fix. She would never give me my freedom as long as she was alive. And since I wasn't flush with cash like I was used to be and wasn't the jerk I could have been, she remained alive and able to walk the planet nearly unimpeded, spending *my* money to take away even more of mine. The lockdowns were having a debilitating effect on doing just every day, routine stuff.

"I know you've thought about putting a bullet into her brain, so don't quote me on it. But some how we have to get rid of her, and I don't mean physically, either, just so we're clear. Doesn't she have something else she likes to do besides make your life Hell?"

"I think if something were to happen to her, everyone in the world would blame me. But honestly, she'd probably rise from the grave and haunt me as well. She has no scruples. None whatsoever. If you ever get some good ideas, shoot them my way, please. Until then, we just have to do it straight up, because if we make a wrong move, she'll pounce on me."

"Just so surprising she would turn on you that way."

"Bob, I did nothing except ask her to leave. Maybe she thought I'd one day come crawling back to her. Ain't ever gonna happen."

"Yeah, and all of us have to keep our distance too."

I thought about Shannon. Maybe I'd have to adjust my standards if she tried to go after her. But hopefully, not.

"So call me tomorrow after you get this banking thing set. Let me know who can give me those records, or I'll have to ask for an extension."

"Get the extension. I've got to go to D.C. Tuesday. Then I'm off to the Indian Ocean for a few days, including travel time."

"The sultan?"

"Yup."

"You should ask his advice. How many wives does he have?"

"I think he's going on thirteen. And yes, I've admired how he can seem to keep his household in shape."

"Well, unlike Rebecca, they don't have much of an alternative."

"I think you're right, Bob. Rebecca has lots of options now that she's gotten the settlement. I'm going to try to get it all back, and then some. But I'm going to do it legally."

"Music to my ears, Marco. You did it once. You can do it again. I'm keeping my ear to the pavement for wind of anything, and I'll let you know. You just go out there trying to patch everything up and I'll fight your battles in court."

I was glad I'd never taken anything out on him personally and still felt bad for how I'd treated Frank. I had deserved that one big time, and I really missed having him at my side.

My cell rang. Harry's familiar voice tried to charm me. He wanted to put the sultan on the line.

I was okay with that.

I was going to ask his advice. I embraced the inevitable that my future was somehow linked with his purely because he was probably the only person on the planet Rebecca couldn't get to.

Maybe that was his secret.

CHAPTER 14

Shannon

I FOUND JARED as soon as I walked into the station.

"I have a problem with the Rebecca Gambini interview."

He was crisply dressed in a white shirt, tie askew. His sleeves were rolled up. He'd been writing something, and as usual, he'd been dunking wads of discarded drafts, mostly hitting the garbage can in the corner.

He sat forward, elbows on the desk, checking his cell phone.

"The interview that's supposed to start in twenty minutes? That what you're talking about?" He eyed me closely, squinting, as if he suspected some change had come over me. Or maybe I was just feeling like I had a big sign on my back that said "I slept with Marco Gambini."

"She's already here, Shannon. She brought you a

coffee. She told me she'd promised it to you."

"Oh God." I mashed my face with my palm.

"That bad? She have a disease of some kind, Shannon?" He wasn't getting any of what I was feeling.

Of course he isn't!

I looked down on him. "I slept with her husband, Jared."

He scratched his chin and fingered his lips, checking down the hallway to make sure no one was listening.

"Tell me why you thought that was a good idea?"

"I *didn't* think. I'm not sorry, but I didn't think."

"Let me see if I have this straight. You're the young lady who wants a career in broadcasting, is that right?"

I nodded.

"You ask for special favors, which I give you. Did you do this *after* or before I helped you get the interview all set up?"

"Both."

He cocked his head to the side as if he was going to knock water out of his ears. "I don't believe I'm hearing this. I once worked for an editor of a small-town newspaper who told me *never* to hire women. Work only with men. I'm beginning to understand why he told me that."

"Jared, I can't interview her. It would be unethical of me."

Jared stood up, walked behind me, and closed his door. He stood no more than a foot away. "No, Shannon, that would be *what you already did!*" He calmed himself and whispered, "I don't give a flying fuck how you manage to justify this little viper's nest of sex, lies, and video tape, but I won't be a part of it. And I'll not save your bacon, either. You're on your own. Get your little buns down to makeup so she can remove that disgusting peachy glow off your face and paint your lips red. Bright red. You Jezebel!"

Him raising his voice knocked some sense into me. He was right. It was all my problem. Why had I even told him? With my back still turned to him, I mumbled an apology and opened his door. As I was leaving I heard his stinging rebuke, controlled and softly spoken.

"You should have had the drink with me. That was the choice you should have made."

I carefully closed the door behind me and heard the crash of something hitting the wall in his tiny office.

Sandy, our makeup gal, took a look at my hair, still wet from the very steamy and soap-lathering love licking and kissing tickle fest in the shower and rolled her eyes. Her Cuban accent was always stronger when she was annoyed.

"Why didn't you just come in soaking? You got parts here that stick straight up and parts here that are limp, see? I cannot do curling iron on you because it will burn your hair. And it's no good to see that on camera, either. So, we leave it?" she said, with her wide, fake smile challenging me in the mirror.

"Yes, I think so. Where is…"

"Ah," she leaned over and whispered in my ear. "That beech I'd like to slap across the face. I do her makeup, all pretty. You know, for the taping? She stares at me and wipes it all off with tissue, smudges her lipstick halfway up to her nose. They gonna think I gave her a bloody lip. You watch out for dat beech."

"I already know about her. Just get some powder and lipstick on me so I don't look like I'm sweating through my clothes, which I am."

"Ya. I do a good job for you. I got a whole two minutes to do a good job for you. You know it takes much longer to do professional makeup."

"Stop it, Sandy, and just get it done. And, say a prayer for me."

She said something in Spanish I didn't understand and crossed herself.

"What did you do to get hooked up with this chica? You musta been a bery, bery bad girl."

"You don't know the half of it."

"So you gonna get your butt spanked today? It going to be a regular catfight with dat one."

"Sandy, this isn't helping. Please, I have to get to

the set.

"Oh, the set! You should see the roses got delivered for the set. Making half the older folks around here sneezing their butts off, too. Roses is too strong I tell you."

"Who are they from? For me?" I was blushing through all the powder she was applying.

"No card. Nothing. I think they were for *her*." Sandy lowered her voice and whispered in my ear, "She musta got one of them gangsta boys or a Don. Someone who's all sorry he got nasty with her. Yea, dat's what I think."

But I knew otherwise. Marco was inserting himself into an already complicated and dangerous situation.

Bunny Copperfield poked her head into the room. "We gotta go, Shannon. Everything's set." Her headsets were falling off the back of her head. She hugged her clipboard to her enormous chest. That was the way she always ran around here, covering herself up.

"She was askin' about the flowers, Bunny. You know anything?" asked Sandy.

"A secret admirer. We teased Rebecca about that."

Except no one else knew she was coming in except the staff here and Marco.

"Come on, Shannon. They're playing the weekend show credits."

"This is live?" My knuckles clutched the metal handles on the black makeup chair.

"Yes. Didn't Jared tell you? She requested it. He said he tried to call you." Bunny pulled my arm and extricated me from the chair. I ran quickly behind her to keep from falling.

The set was different than the normal routine. Hanging in the background was a huge American flag. On the raised dais were two light blue easy chairs, halfway facing one another on either side of a low coffee table with two paper coffee cups. On the table was an enormous glass vase filled with heady deep red roses. I didn't check for a card or note, because if there had been one, I was going to sit on it.

Rebecca came onto the set from the other side. She pointed to my coffee. "I brought you a cappuccino, just like I promised, Shannon."

I was frozen in place. This wasn't happening to me right now because I was somewhere else—anywhere else, floating up to the moon or someplace never to be heard from again.

Bunny whispered, "Sit, ladies! We have to start now."

I collapsed, kinda awkwardly onto one hip, then adjusted myself, pulled my hair behind my ears and over my shoulders, and smiled at the camera after I licked my lips.

They had a teleprompter all ready with my introduction, which I was grateful for and hadn't even thought about. As I focused on the letters, I heard Rebecca clear her throat and then gargle a tiny bit.

It was distracting. I was sure I looked like a cat about to be hit with a broom.

"Good morning, Tampa Bay!"

The canned applause had me looking off into the blackness to see where the audience was.

"We have a very special treat in store for you today. As many of you know, this station supports veterans causes, and when we heard that headway was being made on the new Trident Towers building for disabled Navy SEALs, as well as other at-risk and deserving veterans, we knew you, the viewers, would love to hear more about it. As luck would have it, we have our very own celebrity with us today, Rebecca Gambini, wife to former SEAL Marco Gambini…" My stomach lurched and almost tripped over the fact that they hadn't mentioned they were divorced.

When my introduction was complete and the canned clapping died down, I turned to Rebecca, who smiled back eagerly. I could see a little of the lipstick Sandy was talking about but doubted it would show. She was dressed in red, white and blue. I was in all blue.

"Welcome, Rebecca."

"Thank you, Shannon, for having me. I'm delighted

to be here. Did you sleep well?" She followed it up with a wink.

I froze again. Did she know?

I studied my fingers twisting around themselves in my lap, brushed the hair that had fallen into my eyes, tossing it behind me, and then turned to the camera.

"What Rebecca is referring to is a very pleasant evening we spent together, listening to oldies music and drinking entirely too much wine."

Rebecca beamed. The canned audience laughter was a little late on cue.

"It wasn't wine. We were drinking Scotch," she said, nodding in my direction. To the camera, she announced. "It was one of the funniest girl's night outs I've ever had!"

I quickly jumped in, whispering, "Don't tell my mother. She thinks I only drink wine."

Again, more canned laughter.

"So, Rebecca here is working on the Trident Towers. Tell me about it and what are your plans? How can we help you as a station?"

"Well, thank you. I appreciate that so much. The Trident Towers is part of the mission statement of my husband," she raised her eyebrow and spoke lower, "my *ex*-husband, that is. And don't worry. It was an amicable divorce. In fact, I think he sent these, unless your boyfriend did, Shannon."

My pulse quickened. Either she was living in a fantasy world or she was tooling me. I couldn't tell which one it was, and what complicated it more was that she was right about some of it.

"No, I'm sure they were meant for you, Rebecca," I lied.

"I still enjoy working closely with him on his various philanthropic projects. As wives and family of Navy SEALs, it is often our calling to help heal these heroes when they come home. As I started to tell you, they have a saying, "Leave no man behind," which is throughout all our military as a code of conduct. Some who come home can't take the first step to becoming whole, to healing. They leave it all out on the battlefield and come home empty. We want to show them we love them. That they are not forgotten."

She delivered it well. I put myself in the place I would have been if I hadn't felt Marco pulsing inside me as he held me close—if I had never met him, tasted his kisses, or seen the way he looked at me when we made love with our eyes open.

"Such an honorable and noble plan, Rebecca. And how unselfish of you to carry on your husband's vision, too."

"I think if you really loved someone once, you always do," she answered timidly.

I imagined if Marco were watching the interview

he'd throw something at the set right about now. She was exquisite with the lying and the play acting. Far better than I.

"So when does construction begin, and will all the designs be the same as previously proposed?"

"That's the part I love the best. I should have been an interior decorator. We're picking out colors right now, placing holds on fabric and carpeting. The construction will begin just as soon as the modified plans come out of design review. We have the financing all ready to go. I'd say, by next April? And occupancy on some of the earliest units in the back a year from now. Just in time for Thanksgiving and Christmas."

"Really?"

She nodded, proud of herself.

"What kind of changes are you making to the plans?"

"Well, we've created some group living spaces where several bachelors can live together, share duties. They will be offered at a reduced rental rate. We have small condominium-style apartment homes for purchase, which will of course qualify for VA so the vets can come in with no money down. We've got a scale model prepared for the hearings, and I've brought in a whole new team of sales agents and representatives of the non-profit to help these men and women find the right home for them, based on what they can qualify for. We'll have some that are handicap accessible for some of our disabled veterans."

She made it sound like Shangri-la. I was genuinely impressed at how well thought out the project was. "I'm sure our viewers will be anxious to hear more about it. When you have the interior renderings and color schemes, would you come back and share it again with us all?"

"I'd be happy to, Shannon."

"And how can veterans get in touch with the nonprofit group that is helping to spearhead this?"

"Well, when I took over, I naturally had to make some staffing changes. I have a brilliant general manager working under me and he has charity background, so he's going to handle the sales. Perhaps we can have him come on and share as well. He's smart. He's about your age, Shannon, and he's very cute!"

I couldn't help but blush. I immediately sensed he was her new boyfriend, her new toy. Someone she could torture and make run away.

"I'll leave the contact information so anyone can call the station and get that given to them," she added.

"That would be great!" My voice broke so I grabbed my water.

The ending music began, and I was surprised how quickly the ten minutes had gone by. After I thanked her for her time, we talked out of earshot of the audience. She became fixated on the roses and touched them.

"You are sure your boyfriend didn't...because this looks like..." she started.

"No, ma'am. If he had sent these, there would have been a card. Trust me on that." A nervous giggle erupted from my throat, and then I had a hiccup.

"May I take them with me?"

"Of course. They're yours, Rebecca."

She eagerly grabbed the huge vase, peeked around the bouquet and asked, "Care to join me for a bite to eat?"

"No, thanks. I have some things here I have to work on for the weather report later on."

"Dinner?"

"My boyfriend, remember?"

"Oh yes. Well, maybe tomorrow then. If you're free."

"I'm going to play it by ear. He has to leave on—" I hesitated giving too much detail. "I think he'll be here until Thursday, and I want as much time with him as possible. Thank you so much for doing this, Rebecca."

"I enjoyed it."

CHAPTER 15

Marco

THE BENTLEY WAS to arrive soon, so I quickly showered. I thought about the phone call I had with sultan Bonin earlier today. It went well, which is to say I gave him everything he wanted. In return, he got *me*. He didn't want anyone else. He wanted me. And he would have paid double what he offered me. It was an insane amount of money.

So I light-heartedly asked him for his advice on the woman front.

"My biggest problem, son."

"Oh really? Because everyone looks pretty happy to me."

"You are not family. With family, they fight like cats and dogs."

"So how do you keep the peace, then?"

"By never expecting it to change. Now, when my affairs of the heart get in the way of my duties as administrator of our tiny kingdom, my ministers' step in, and that's when it can get ugly."

"You love them all?"

He chuckled, then fell into a coughing fit that concerned me. "If they are blowing on my balls and sucking my staff, yes, I fall in love. I like to fall in love several times a day. But you, Marco, you are at a very great disadvantage. You should have been raised in our part of the world. You could have—"

"I never wanted more than one woman at a time. That's where we're different."

"Ah, so you have been bitten hard by the snake of love. Then it is simple. You will feel much pain and be miserable until the day you die."

It was my time to laugh. I nearly spit out my coffee.

"Haven't you learned by now how to ignore them? I've seen pictures of you guys running on the beach. You don't grab the pretty ladies who like to show themselves to you and take them in the waves, do you? You focus on your mission, and that is why what you offer is a gift greater than happiness, than all the wealth of the world. Me? I don't have that. I learned my lesson. I fell in love with Harry's mother. I could never make her my wife, but she was the wife of my heart. It was her face I saw when I was bedding my wives. I saw little Harry's tiny face when I greeted my other children and grandchildren into the world. And because of that, I had to move her away from the palace, or both their lives could be at risk."

"You see her?"

"It was a long time ago, Marco. I don't want to see her now. She was the sweetest flower of all the land. I want to remember her that way. My seeing her would be dangerous for her. I had to cut out those feelings with a sharp knife, because it was my love that would cause her death."

"Fascinating. We are polar opposites."

"So why all this talk of managing harems you will never have? Sounds like perhaps you are in love with two women at the same time?"

"No, not really. I thought I was in love when I was married. But now I don't know what it was. It was like I was running away from something. I needed something from her for a time, and then when I stopped needing it, somehow, we just ended. The fun and excitement were gone. She's probably right. I was the one who walked away, even though she was the one who was unfaithful."

"Women are complicated. You ignore them. You let them go. You bury your happy memories if you have to, but you let them go find someone else. And then you pretend to be happy for them. You see? That's how it works."

"So I shouldn't have gotten angry when she sued

me for divorce and took away half my fortune—or more?"

"Mmmm. I see, young Marco. You didn't fix this soon enough. What were you doing, this running away?"

"I was driven to become a success. And the woman I loved, I made her wait too long."

"Go back and get her, Marco. And tell these two other women who are fighting over you to—how do they say it, 'put your big panties on?' The sultan laughed until he began the coughing spell again.

"Are you sure you are well?"

"Who cares? I am in pain, and I know there are things inside me that are not right. But as long as I can still fuck, I'm alive. In my mind, I go someplace else, and I cavort with all the nubile virgins who I haven't tried yet."

Maybe the sultan was right. I was running from Rebecca, who wouldn't let go. I was running into the arms of someone new. Perhaps I'd been running away from the one I should have married, my dear, sweet Emily. And I couldn't go get her because she was gone forever.

"You are too pensive. I don't like you pensive, Marco. I wish my sons had as much honor and commitment as you have in your little finger. I wish they thought more about their choices and the consequences of those choices. You're too hard on yourself."

"You're probably right. But my problem is that the first one I loved is no longer walking this planet."

"Yes, I think Harry told me about this. I am so sorry for you. So you cannot repair things with your wife, or is the new girlfriend too much of a temptation to walk away from?"

"Neither. Rebecca, my ex-wife, won't leave me alone, even though I left years ago. And now she's bitter, spiteful, and making my life miserable."

"You will really have a problem when she learns about the new one."

"She won't."

He laughed again, this time surviving without the coughs. "Women always find out. You be careful. Your new one is tough?"

"She's strong, not tough. I don't need tough. I need to feel like I did when I had Emily. She's very much like her, in certain ways. In other ways, no. Emily was simple. She wouldn't have cared about all the money I made or what kind of a house we lived in. In a way, I don't think she would have loved the man I became when I was married to Rebecca. And all Rebecca wants to do is take everything away from me."

"Ask the favor you are afraid to ask, my son. I see no easy doorways open to you."

"No, I'll think of something."

"Marco, you need a loyal friend who can play in your sandbox. You are going to help me with these kids of mine and their project in Africa. I don't care if they lose money. I just don't want them killed in the process. They don't see danger all around them. They still think they're in Disneyland. I send them to schools. They are indulged, fancy boys who make horrible decisions and even father children from low caste women. And why? They could have all the beauties they want. But no, they want the common girls, the street urchins. Why, I'll never know."

"Well, I understand that a little, I guess. They want to do it on their own. I hope that they don't realize too late what a gift having you for a father is to them. You are their greatest fan, their silent ally."

"Ally! That's the word I was looking for. So. Marco. How can I help you? I want to be your ally."

I wasn't proud of it, but he was offering his hand. "I need a miracle, sultan."

"Done. You tell Harry how much."

"How did you know I wasn't going to ask you to get rid of my wife?"

"Because, Marco, you would never do that. You'd die first. And that's why you are going to protect my sons. I won't murder for you, but money? I can do money."

THE STATION WAS just about to air Shannon's interview when I got the call that the car had arrived. I slipped on some shorts and flip flops and dashed downstairs shirtless, doing a skidding stop on the smooth marble floor of the Oceanis grand lobby. I felt I was playing Poseidon in a movie or something, with all the colorful larger-than-life mermaids and sea creatures suspended from the multi-storied ceiling and depicted in beautiful stained-glass windows that gave the feeling of being under water. I was hoping I could get back upstairs and watch the news in time to see Shannon's program.

When my forward movement stopped, I noticed I'd attracted quite a bit of attention. A couple of ladies sitting in the bar gave me a loud whistle and a toast, already smashed at ten in the morning.

I took my bow, and ran outside to behold my new toy. It was cherry apple red—the most brilliant red I'd ever seen, that lipstick "I'm in trouble" kind of red, or the red a naughty girl would wear to church. The ivory and caramel leather interior was stunning. No one would ever mistake this beast for the cockpit of an airplane, and that was why I loved it so. Light Ash dash, heavily grained, made a gorgeous contrast to the sleek lines and tan colored top, which was down, of course. She looked dripping wet for me. I was going to have so much fun in this baby.

"Mr. Gambini?" A tall, handsome twenty-something kid came toward me wearing one of Tony's white polo shirts with the Bentley logo on it, extending his hand to give me the keys.

"You won't really need these, but you might have to valet park. Come on and let's get your thumbprint recorded, shall we?"

He looked like he was having as much fun as I was. I pressed my thumb against a tiny square piece of what looked like glass embedded in the shiny chrome of the driver's handle. His fingers pressed tightly on top until the few seconds passed and a discrete beep came from somewhere on the dash, indicating my fingerprint had been stored.

"So if someone wanted to steal this car, they'd have to bring me with them, right?" I barked, turning heads in the entrance.

The kid had a healthy laugh, showing perfectly straight and brilliant white teeth. "Well, your thumb, at least. And if it's detached, before it gets too wrinkly."

It was funny. The kid was okay. I immediately wondered if he needed a job, since everyone was quitting these days.

I focused back on my new ride. "Can I take it for a spin?"

"Of course, sir. She's all yours. You want me to show you all the bells and whistles?"

"I guess I can be patient. How long will this take?"

"Seriously? About forty-five minutes." He didn't flinch, so I knew he was telling me the truth.

About halfway through the demonstration, Corrine, the pretty concierge, came running out with her arms full of beautiful camel-colored blankets with the distinctive *swimming O* that was the logo for the hotel embroidered in blue at one corner.

"Pop the trunk, and I'll place these inside," she said with a confident grin.

I hit the wrong toggle and started the windshield wipers, getting water on the leather front seats. She handed the stack of blankets to me and quickly rubbed the seats down with one of the monogrammed towels she had also brought.

"I'll just get you another, Mr. Gambini," she gushed, covering up my misstep.

"I'm so sorry. I guess I should have paid more attention."

The delivery salesman pressed a button on the key fob, and the trunk popped open slowly without making a sound. Inside was a matching set of his and hers luggage pieces, made from the same darker accent leather on the interior, so it tastefully matched the car. He found a space between the two pieces and laid the blankets down.

Corrine was running off to the lobby area and as an afterthought, turned and waved at me. "Don't go away.

I have something else to show you. Wait right there!" She was jumping like an oversized piece of popcorn.

The salesman completed his instruction, showed me the compartment where the leather-bound car manual was located. Tony had provided him with my insurance information, so that was tucked inside. The booklet holding everything was embossed with my initials, MG.

Corrine came clickety clacking down the entrance steps, taking what sounded like little bird hops, carrying a wicker basket with a bottle of champagne nestled inside, surrounded by fresh towels.

"It has no ice, just gel packs, which you can re-freeze and re-use."

"Or, you can store them in your little cooler in your trunk, Mr. Gambini," Tony's guy said.

"You have to be kidding me?" she gasped. "You have a refrigerator in your car? That's amazing. You could drive from here to San Francisco and never have to stop for cold beer!"

Under her arm, she held another folded fluffy white towel to replace the one she'd used on the seats. They had my initials on them as well.

"I guess you can steal the towels here, Marco," said the kid.

I knew I'd already missed Shannon's show and figured she might have saved me a clip. I really didn't want to think about Rebecca, anyway. I hadn't brought my license so Paul, the young salesman, accompanied me on the test run.

When I pushed the button, the thing growled and idled like the racehorse she was. I commanded her with both hands on the steering wheel, released the brake, and away we went. The car's pedal was going to take some getting used to, featherly light and so sensitive. I was getting turned on by how little I had to do to get such a complete monster reaction out of her. We drove down Gulf Blvd., turning heads everywhere. She wanted the freeway, but I wanted to treat her to a nice tree-lined pasture for her maiden voyage. She cornered perfectly.

She was going to be my second love.

I couldn't wait to show her off at sunset.

I left the keys with the concierge, who squealed with delight. "I want roses tucked in two bouquets on the rear seat floor, the champagne in the middle."

"Oh, and I've found some to-die-for grouper bites, too, and some blackened shrimp. I'll put some grapes in there as well. I didn't have time to get the flutes monogrammed, sorry to say."

I kissed her on her cute little forehead. "Go make me proud, Corrine!"

"What time will you arrive?"

I checked my cell. "She is supposed to meet me at

six. I've got the right spot picked out for our little picnic."

"Leave it to me, Mr. Gambini. And you'll want roses in the suite as well? Some midnight snacks in the refrigerator? More champagne chilled in a bucket?"

"Perfect. I'm hiring a car to go pick her up, so you can get the red-head ready. We should be here no later than six-thirty, but I'll text you."

"Oh, Mr. Gambini," she said, her hand clasped under her chin, "You are such a romantic. She's a lucky girl."

"I'm the lucky one."

I WAS AT her house when she arrived home, using the key she left for me in a flower pot. I'd taken the time to study every piece of her artwork carefully. I didn't want to pry, but something about this woman was a mystery, as if we'd been connected in another life.

And I never believed in such things.

"Is that your car outside?" she asked as she ran to me.

"Of course it is. He's waiting to take you to your surprise." We kissed. She smelled so good, and with the good news I had with the sultan, I felt free to just enjoy her lovely body, her happy spirit. It was one of the things I did need from her. And I'd always been a man who didn't need anything from anyone.

"So how did it go?"

"You didn't watch?" She wrinkled her forehead, disappointed.

"I'm sorry, but I had something that I had to do. But you'll get a copy of it, won't you?"

"Yes. I just hope that you're not upset when you watch it."

"Why would that be?" I said as she folded into my arms.

"At first, I thought she was just going after this project because it was something you felt strongly about. Now? I actually think she wants to do it. She's hard to figure out. Could you ever see your way to letting her take it over?"

"Never."

"But if she left you alone?"

"I don't know what it would take to have her leave me alone."

She laced a forefinger over my lips. "I think she needs a job in life. Maybe she just wants to prove to you that she can do big projects."

"She can't." I separated us, walking over toward the kitchen, rubbing the back of my neck. "And I'm done talking about her."

My words must have been too strong because Shannon looked like she was about to burst into tears. I crossed the room like a flash, took her into my arms and rocked her. "I'm sorry. That came out wrong."

She broke away from me this time. "Give her a chance, Marco."

"Maybe I better see the video before I answer that."

"Fair enough. I can live with that."

SHE QUICKLY SHOWERED and changed into a very low-cut black cocktail dress and some sparkly sandals that highlighted her slender ankles and beautiful, long legs. She wore a brightly colored scarf for a wrap, and as the car drove up the ten miles of beach homes, I could see that we were nearly out of time to watch the sunset, but we'd make it.

When we pulled into the Oceanis entrance, we scattered a flock of flamingos who were crossing the approach. We stopped just behind the beautiful cherry red Bentley convertible. I pulled her from the back seat, and sent the driver off. The bellman came running, bringing me the keys.

"Sir, we were afraid you weren't coming. You didn't text."

"I was so happy seeing my girl I completely forgot." Shannon smiled back at both of us.

"Ready to take her for a spin?"

"This? This is yours?"

"Yes, ma'am, and you're going to drive us. Can you do that?"

Shannon curled down her lower lip. "Is it a stick shift?"

"Nope. Automatic. Twelve cylinders of pure cherry-flavored pussy."

I loved seeing her blush. I helped her into the driver's seat and strapped her in.

"Marco, it has champagne. I don't want to spill it, and flowers. OMG, there are dozens of roses here. Did—"

I stopped her with a kiss. "Yes, I sent them. Did you like them?"

She didn't answer.

We headed up Gulf Blvd. until I found the beach access road I was looking for. She carefully drove the lush green jungle trail until we came to the clearing on a vacant lot I owned. I instructed her to face the car toward the street and aim the rear at the beach and ocean.

"Come on," I said, running to her side. I unlocked the trunk and pulled out the blankets, handing them to her, then brought the wicker basket with the treats and the champagne. I pulled her up over the dunes, and we lay the blankets on the white sand, sat and watched the orange globe of the sun begin to set. Everywhere we looked the sky was orange and purple. A warm breeze blew off the bay as I sat behind her, holding her in my arms.

"I never get tired of this view. It's the best thing about my little bungalow."

"Agreed. You have one of the best views. Tiny house but big view."

"No one's here."

"I know. That's why I chose it."

The sun hung so low it nearly touched the water as I poured her glass and watched the bright orange glow in her face and shoulders, the way her eyes sparkled, the way she smiled at me.

"To us, Shannon. I made this sunset for us."

"To us."

She touched her glass to mine, took a sip, and watched the sun disappear.

I parted the towels and found some still-warm cheese biscuits and grouper bites, which were amazing. They'd put grapes and strawberries in there, along with cheeses and some crackers. She fed me, and I sucked her fingers if she wasn't quick enough.

It was beginning to chill with the sun having set, but the air was still streaked with color. The waves washed the beach clean as birds ran over the smooth sand foraging for food.

"Wanna try something with me?" I asked.

"Now you have me intrigued. I could sit here all night. It's so beautiful."

"You can see it a little better from the car, Shannon.

And I can turn the heater on, if you like. And it will smell like roses."

Her dancing eyes told me she was game.

We gathered everything up and walked the tiny dunes trail to the car. I removed one of the vases of roses and the holder that was keeping them balanced and placed it on the ground. I pushed the seat forward, spread two blankets on the floor and the seat and directed her to kneel so she could see the view.

I poured us each another glass of champagne and joined her. Bringing another blanket up to her shoulders, I whispered between nibbling kisses, "Take your panties off, Shannon."

She set her finished glass on the floor and blew back to me, "I'm not wearing any, Marco." I let her remove my glass and then work on my pants buckle, unbuttoning my shirt as she did so. Her cool fingers slipped down the front where she gently squeezed my package. Her eyes didn't divert from mine. Her tongue touched my lips, then my extended tongue until the kiss deepened and that glorious rush of adrenaline came over me.

I palmed her bare ass, rubbing her up and down, then let one hand press between her thighs in front to touch her where she wanted to be touched.

Holding her by the waist, I sat her sweet little bottom on the folded canvas top, and parted her knees. I could still see her lips, swollen, abused, and about to be used some more. Two fingers slipped inside her as she moaned and leaned back, resting her torso on the canvas. I removed her sandals one at a time, kissing her up the inside of her legs until my tongue found the warm, pulsing folds of succulent flesh. She pressed one foot against the headrest of the driver side and slid back farther, spreading her knees wider.

Her dress slipped off in my hands. Then I slowly suckled, kissed, and penetrated her with my tongue.

"Oh, God, Marco! I'm going to come in your mouth already."

"Yes, Shannon. Give it to me."

Her sweet juices covered my lips, my chin and my nose. I nipped her clit with my teeth and she went wild with need. I savored and watched her squeeze her breasts, then sit up and hold my fingers as I entered her over and over again until she drew my face up to hers and took from me a long, lingering kiss.

I carefully turned her over, her glowing ass making me hard just looking at it. Her elbows rested on the top. I rubbed her sex and then gave her space to think about what was coming next while I removed my shirt. I plucked one of the roses and let it tickle her from her neck to her anus. I crushed the flower and allowed the petals to fall all over her nude body now being illuminated by moonlight. My pants fell to my knees as I stood on the seat, kneeled slightly and pressed her body against the car. I positioned my cock so she could feel how engorged I was. I rubbed my tip over the crease in her ass, probing, sliding and then finally entering between her fluttering labia. Holding her hips, I pulled her back and onto me, rocked her with my thighs, allowing her to straddle my lap, and then rammed inside deep as if I could split her in two.

Our tongues played as we kissed from the side. I spread her cheeks, and moved deeper still. Her behind pressed against me for full penetration, her feet at my sides as I pumped her, picking up the pace until her long rolling orgasm completely overtook her. I grabbed her hips, pulling her to me as I spilled. And then we paused, listening to the sounds of the ocean and the birds who came out to feed.

With the sky turning gray and the ocean chill invading the bluff, we gathered our things, put the top up, and returned to my motel.

I knew I was going to remember this night forever. I was hoping that she would too, when she turned her head and whispered, "Marco, I never want this to end."

I was going to do everything I could to make sure it wouldn't.

CHAPTER 16

Shannon

I WOKE UP with a headache and briefly calculated how much champagne I'd consumed—we'd consumed—and took in a deep breath. I was alone in the bed, covered in rose petals. Some of them were caught in the strands of my hair splayed all over the pillow.

I took stock of what the night had been like, both of us unable to sleep because just about every flesh on flesh turn of our bodies created another sensual experience, if not a full-on intense lovemaking session. Overwhelmed was the word that described me perfectly. My stomach churned. My heartbeat was still racing because my libido had been amped up so often it was stuck on full tilt.

I brushed his pillow where his head had been then grabbed it and pushed it against my face, inhaling his strong, masculine scent laced with an exotic cologne

I'd gotten so used to. I couldn't get enough of him.

I was lost.

We'd whispered many things to each other in the early morning hours, and yet I was careful not to sound too smitten. But the truth was I was drowning in pheromones for this man, and it would be a mistake to be the first one to utter the words "I love you." But that's how my heart sang no matter how much I tried to stuff it down.

My experience with men was seriously lacking, but I knew that he was volatile enough to go through heavy mood swings, and because of his current financial situation, he'd be more vulnerable to this now. I didn't want to be one more problem he had to deal with. I could be patient if I wanted that chance for the brass ring.

With the interview with Rebecca, I'd already caused problems enough.

I wanted to be his calm before the storm, the someone he could reach out to and trust, even while I harbored that deep secret of my past and how it intermingled with his from so many years ago. I guess I was lucky he didn't remember. No chance I'd ever forget it, and no chance I would ever be able to recover from all this, either.

Somehow, I'd find a way to tell him. He was a man who deserved as well as needed the truth. I. Would.

Do. This.

I heard him talking on the phone in the living room, so I slipped on an Oceanis white cotton robe, cinched up my waist, passed on the logo slippers, and padded out to the living room barefoot to find him. I grabbed my phone on the way and, as I approached, took pictures of his back as he sat on the arm of the couch, legs crossed, looking out at the ocean.

I walked around him to block his view, still taking pictures. He frowned until I opened the sash of my robe and let my body do the talking. I began filming his expression as more of my body was revealed. He uncrossed his legs, lost his place, and stumbled to finish a sentence.

His eyes were filled with lust as I moved slowly towards him, slipped my robe off my shoulders, and then kneeled in front of him.

He was desperately trying to end his conversation, which made my ministrations all the more exciting for me. I discreetly turned off and placed my phone at my side and let my fingers walk up from his knees to his hardening cock, spreading the robe over his knees to look at what I'd created.

With his eyes closed, he tried to concentrate. "So you've got it all set up, then? And he'll—*argh.*" He gasped as my lips and tongue played with the tip of him. I looked up, watching his eyes as I took one long lap of my tongue from his stem to his tip.

He suddenly gasped.

I could hear whomever was on the other end of the line ask him if everything was okay.

"Yes. Yesss," he hissed as I took him into my mouth all the way until my lips were pressed against his lower belly. He tried to continue. "I'm just so taken with the view from up here. It's incredible." He leaned over and let his hand slip down my spine, traveling clear to my butt crack and then smooth over my buttocks, giving me a silent paddle. "It's so fine," he whispered. And then he sat up and signed off the call.

He threw his phone on the couch. "I hope you didn't tape any of that?"

"Just the part before I slipped off my robe," I said, licking his tip and running it over my lips. "I hope I didn't embarrass you too much."

"You are soooo bad, Shannon," he howled, standing, picking me up and throwing me over his shoulder. He spanked my ass several times on the way to the bedroom.

He spanked deliciously hard.

"Ouch!" I howled.

He threw me on the bed and shook his head as well as his right forefinger.

"You deserved every one of those, and you know you did. You are a naughty. Little. Girl," he enunciated as he climbed up to join me, brushing rose petals to the side.

I stubbornly kept my legs tight together as he tried to separate my thighs. I watched him struggle, my hands above my head, fiddling with my hair. My stomach undulated and teased him, as I acted absent-minded. I pretended to fight him off, all the while needing him to consume me one more time. His cock was red and huge this morning, engorged since our last encounter.

He finally got my knees to separate and I arched up, feet planted on the bed, giving him full access.

"Oh, baby. You are so swollen. Did I do that to you?" He mocked concern, frowning.

"You did, and I liked it."

"Poor thing. Look at how pink and"—he dipped his head and lapped my sex—"hot you are. I'd say feverish."

I felt the jolt from his touch all the way up my spine. Something in my stomach lurched.

"Fix it," I whispered. I let him see the desperation in my face.

His eyes sparkled with the birth of an idea. He held up one finger and ran to the kitchen and pulled something out of the freezer. When he returned, he had the gel pack in one hand and a leftover champagne bottle in the other.

"Hold still. Doctor Marco is going to fix it for you, sweetheart." He held the frozen but still soft gel pack against my flaming lips and pressed. At first, I felt nothing, due to the swelling, but all of a sudden my insides began to spasm and react to the cold.

Discarding the gel pack on the floor, he opened the champagne, took a swig, and then tipped it over, and poured it all over my lips. He lapped and poured, poured and lapped, letting the champagne also drip down his chin onto his chest.

"You want some?" he asked, his eyes wide and dangerous.

I nodded, raising my head to accept the cool bubbly liquid. My ass was sitting in champagne-soaked sheets. My boobs glistened as he did a pour-over and sucked my nipples. The pulsing inside me continued. He drank the rest of the bottle, letting it roll off the bed and onto the carpet.

I was insane for him to be inside me. "Marco, please," I begged.

He fingered my folds again, gently pinching my clit. "You want this, don't you?"

I nodded again, breathing hard and licking my lips, loving how he rimmed and penetrated my opening.

His motions were gentle as he adjusted his upper torso forward, taking hold of my wrists high above my head with one hand and pressing his warm cock at my cool entrance with the other. Slowly, he pushed his way inside, watching me, watching how wide my eyes got, watching my breasts rise and fall as he stretched and massaged my throbbing parts. He rubbed my nub gently and breached my entry, violating me so lovingly. I felt my muscles immediately close down around him. I arched, pressing my breasts to his chest. He kept my hands immobilized but lifted my left knee to above his shoulder, angled to the side and pressed deeper and then deeper until he was knocking on the door of my sweet spot.

His slow hip movements, expertly riding me and playing my body like an instrument replaced the throbbing pain with pure pleasure. His back and forth was slow, deliberate. There was no urgency to any of it, as his gentle rhythm grew my arousal slowly.

This was all about me, and he made no mystery of it as he watched my face and my body react to him. I writhed against the constraint of his fingers gripping my wrists, so I could fully enjoy the capture.

Several minutes later, my internal muscles suddenly clamped down on him, causing me to suck in a deep breath. I exhaled and sank into the wonderful rolling orgasm, leaving my body shaking.

"Oh, baby. You are so beautiful. Look at that," he whispered.

He plunged in and then held himself as I continued

to spasm, falling over the edge of my quick little orgasm like a leaf over a waterfall. And then I felt the familiar pulsing as we both stopped moving and experienced the full impact of our union.

I had never felt so loved. I would never recover from what he'd done to me, both to my body and to my heart.

I was lost forever.

WE ATE BREAKFAST in the fern and palm tree courtyard dining area filled with filtered morning sunlight. I was still reeling from the emotional love-making session that preceded our dangerous shower. I couldn't stop smiling, looking down at my lap, almost embarrassed at how intimate and persistent Marco was with me.

I felt cherished.

I also felt a twinge of sadness that I was having an experience that perhaps should have belonged to my sister. And yet, I wondered if their relationship was somehow different from what I was feeling now.

I could tell he was studying me from across the table.

"You're awfully quiet, Shannon." He took my hand across the table and smiled.

"I have no words. I'm a reporter, well, a weather girl," I said as I tossed my head from side to side, "and I have no words. That's kind of funny, don't you think?"

"You mean like me not doing something because I'd be afraid it would be dangerous?" he tried.

"Yes." I leaned forward, putting both elbows on the table. "I never expected this. To—" I was going to say, "to feel this way" but stopped myself.

He was showing his confusion, his brow furrowed.

I understood now why Emily was so upset when Marco postponed their marriage until his next deployment was over. Almost as if she knew she didn't have much time left. I did have time. I just didn't want him to go. I continued.

"I guess I'm regretting how I'll feel when you've left our sunny state."

He paused, still holding my hand. "Then come with me to Boston, Shannon. You could even find work there if you wanted."

I didn't want to go to Boston as his extra piece of luggage. I wanted what I had here, and I never expected to feel so torn.

"No, Marco, I can't do that."

"You visited me once. You could come again. You have friends there, right? Some other reason you came to Boston?"

This was the question I didn't want to address. I wasn't ready.

"I just felt like it."

He angled his head. "Did you come to see me?"

I had to lie. "Not entirely. My friend told me about this Bachelor Towers place where women weren't supposed to own apartments. I had to see for myself because it sounded so backward. But when I read an article about who lived at the Towers, and saw that you were one of them, well, with your project here in my little sleepy town in Florida, I had to see who this man was."

I didn't want to look him in the eyes because I was afraid he'd see the truth. I'd just dug my hole a little deeper. Would there ever be a way I could extricate myself out of this and keep us together?

"I hate the press. They can be so cruel. And you know, you can't trust much of what you read."

"I'm with you there, Marco."

"So about my leaving, I have to go early tomorrow morning. I've got some business things to attend to and fix a wire transfer that I found out this morning didn't happen. I can't do that from here. And then Tuesday I go to D.C. If Boston is too soon, why don't you meet me there, then?"

"Washington, D.C.?"

He nodded. He wasn't pushing. I was flattered with his persistence.

Relieved we'd gotten off the subject of my first trip to Boston, I smiled. "You know the answer to that. I have to work, but thank you, Marco."

"Then quit."

"I don't *want* to quit. I like my job, most days. And I like the warmth of Florida. The beach, the tropical breezes. It's sort of exotic to me, a mixture of Mexico and the Caribbean. I feel at peace and at home here."

He nodded. "Someone asked me yesterday if you were tough, and I told him no. But I was wrong. You are very tough."

Ask me a different question, Marco. Tell me something I can count on.

I was proud of myself, until he asked me another question.

"Okay. I'm going to try one more time. Come with me to India, to the sultan's palace. That's exotic. You can smell the spices in the air. Beautiful beaches, blue water. His Pink Pasha actually sits on an atoll with coral pink sand. They import flamingos so you'll feel right at home. Imagine wandering around the palace at midnight. The stars never looking brighter. Torches flaring. Beautiful silks and tapestries blowing in the breeze. Opulence you wouldn't believe. You could use it as background for a news story about traveling to exotic lands."

"And when are you going?"

"I have to be there in five days. I'll be done in three, maybe four days, to meet with his sons and their team, but he'll want me to stay longer. Why don't you fly to Boston first and we'll fly out together? It's a long flight, but on a private jet, it's way more fun." He wiggled his eyebrows.

I found it hard not to blush. My heart was fluttering at his beautiful descriptions of a place I knew nothing about. I agreed it would be an interesting trip, to learn about those lands and cultures, since my cultural exposure was so limited. It was very tempting.

I decided to split the difference, keep the door open but make sure I wasn't something he intended to drape across his arm. I didn't want to be a harem princess. The train had already left the station and I wanted to see where it went. I hoped to contribute somehow. I never wanted to be a restricted bird in a golden cage.

Marco would have never liked that, either. Why did he expect that I would?

"I'll ask for time off. I'll ask for a week, ten days, and I'll try to give you an answer today. But I don't want you to be angry at me if I won't quit my job to do it."

"I understand."

He held out his hand, and we left to attend his project meeting. Our plan was that he was going to take me home and then pick me up again for dinner. He'd already told me he wanted to retire early. So that gave me an idea.

"About dinner, Marco. Why don't I make you something at my place? If you're comfortable, you can spend the night, or come back here. But it's up to you."

"What would *you* like?"

I waved my hands out above my head. "This is beautiful. It really is. But I like my little place better. I like hearing the ocean. I like to cook. You've shown me how you live. Let me show you how I live, what I like to do in that little space. I don't need all this. I'd like you to stay with me before you go."

It took a few seconds for it to thoroughly sink in. "Okay, we'll do that. If that's what you want, that's what we'll do."

"Thank you."

"For what?"

"For listening to me, for understanding what's important to me. Not everything in my world is about money."

He was silent for a moment, and then he said something that brought tears to my eyes.

"You remind me of someone I used to love a long time ago. She passed away way too soon, unfortunately. But I suddenly miss her."

"I understand."

And I did.

CHAPTER 17

Marco

THE OFFICIAL BONE Frog Development group sat on mismatched office chairs we'd secured from thrift stores, along with several desks and some file cabinets in beige and sand colors. Our rented office was one block from the construction site, in a repurposed gas station. It wasn't fancy, but it was cheap space, and the group had shown their creative genius by fixing it up with a great sound system, bright colors, and eclectic artwork. I found some of my old things I lent to them as well.

My loosely labeled manager, Rhea, and her partner had designated themselves as leaders of this little conclave, the "mother hens" so to speak. They were fiercely loyal, and I liked that they were invested in the project and loved bossing people around. But they were effective at it, not abusive. The team we'd hired together loved them both. Each of them had a different style, which worked well. I couldn't have made it with just one without the other. Between their talent and their management style, it was a winning combination. I also felt they had my back.

Between the two, Rhea was the one who didn't have a problem speaking her mind, whereas Dax, her partner, was the soft touch and the person who smoothed over ruffled feathers. Rhea had been born into a military family and had lived all over the world, and she'd served as a communications officer in the Marines for ten years. The only person she reported to was me, but she didn't mind co-managing the group with her lifelong girlfriend.

"It isn't about the money, Marco. It's that you backed out on your promise, man," Rhea barked. "I never thought we'd have to face this, Boss."

I could see we had more of a problem than I'd calculated. I knew I should have been on it sooner. "But I didn't do it. Rebecca did."

Rhea had a small contracting company doing remodels. She hired mostly women carpenters, plumbers, and electricians. It made it so much easier that I didn't have to worry about little construction defects or issues at the space, because Rhea and her ladies could fix anything. I was counting on some grant money for having such a large female staff and hoped I could award the buildout to them. Rhea could also do material takeoffs faster than anyone I'd ever met since she knew how to read plans.

"I'm not abandoning the project. I can't battle everything at once, guys. I've made a promise. It isn't going back on my word. I have to do this strategically."

She didn't like it, but she seemed to accept it. I caught her eyeing Shannon several times and knew I'd have to make a private, formal introduction or there would be gossiping going on all over the place.

One of the new hires I didn't recognize, who was wheelchair bound, added, "We do appreciate the extra, but I gotta get a job. I can't wait around to find out if I got a permanent job."

Rhea pointed over her shoulder with her thumb. "He's reception."

"I may not have legs, but I'll bet I can climb a ladder faster than you!"

The group laughed and I was grateful for the lightheartedness. I hadn't seen him do that, but with my experience in several foreign countries, I'd seen people do amazing things without the use of their legs, and climbing ladders was one of them.

"Look, guys, I got it." I was truly sorry for having brought them together, gotten them so excited about what we could do, even with the divorce raging, without it occurring to me that my personal life would affect theirs. I fully intended to make it up to them, and told them so. I asked for their patience and to trust me.

Almost no one believed me. The groans and whispered swear words were frequent and disturbing.

"I thought you had the financing all set up, Marco," someone asked.

"It got pulled. I had a note called, part of my divorce attorney battle, and it caught me completely off guard. But I've secured the replacement, so all will be good."

"Except she's going around town telling everyone she's in charge. So what does that make us?" someone else commented.

"We're the barnyard animals," countered Rhea.

It bothered me that these people, who had so little, had shown their loyalty to me and I was in danger of letting them down. Somehow, I'd get this thing back on track and turn it into the flagship I knew it could be.

"And that's the problem. I can't stop that as fast as I can make sure you get paid," I added.

"For how long?" one of the big guys asked. I knew he'd also been a Marine. "I got a kid and a wife. I gotta get a job, Marco. Unlike you, this isn't a hobby."

I did understand, but they obviously felt like the little guys, the ones who always got the shaft. I was going to make sure that didn't happen.

"I'll promise you'll get paid for at least two months, maybe three. We still have work to do. We collected a pretty sizeable list of possible donors. Those people have to be contacted. And we have the suggested recipients. Rhea, you said you wanted to work on the standards. Everybody's needs will be different, depending on their situation. Most of the project will be guys, but we had a family unit set up. I don't know what she's doing about that, since she's having some changes done. But our work isn't done."

More groans erupted from my group.

"Someone is going to have to go over to the Design Review office and find out what changes they are proposing. I understand they aren't approved yet, and I guess I'll be forced to speak with Rebecca, through her attorney, of course."

I didn't see much hope in their eyes.

"Why doesn't *she* ask her?" Kevin, a twenty-something with full sleeves asked, pointing to Shannon. "They're buddy-buddy. She's the weather girl, Shannon Marr."

"Not really," corrected Shannon. "It was just an interview and probably a one-off at that."

"But you could ask," suggested Rhea, giving her a respectful wink. I could see Shannon wasn't entirely comfortable with her.

Shannon looked at me, and I gently shook my head. It was a bad idea.

"I'm not sure she's still in town, anyway," she answered. "But I'd be willing to try, if you think it would help, Marco."

God dammit. This is the last thing I need.

"I don't want you anywhere around her." I stopped all the crosstalk that had erupted with my voice rising over their chattering. "The checks will be couriered here tomorrow—for all of you. You'll get checks every Monday for at least two months. You can count on that."

I asked Rhea and her partner to meet me in the back, out of earshot of the rest of the group. Shannon joined us.

Rhea looked her up and down. "Hey Boss, do I have to train my replacement?"

"I couldn't replace you, Rhea." I pulled Shannon over to my side, wrapping my arm around her waist. "This is personal. Very personal. And none of your goddamned business, either."

Rhea chuckled, and Dax looked relieved. "Nice to meet you, Shannon," she said.

"You ladies are in a perfect position to try to get yourselves hired over on Rebecca's crew. If you do, and you report back to me, you'll still get your salary here, too. But I want just the two of you to go first. I need to know if she's really serious about the buildout."

"Boss, I don't understand why you don't just talk to her. Work something out," said Rhea.

"So she can screw me again? I wouldn't give her the satisfaction. I'm going to be gone for about two weeks. During that period of time, divide everyone who's staying into groups and put someone in charge of each one. One group can contact donors. Another can interview the vets who responded to the interest post card. I want the team leader of that one to interview every single one of them. Go to their houses. Get a sense of what they really need. We'll start with this group, make a list of their needs, and then adjust from there. I need to know what handicaps we're building for."

"Did you have the trees cut down?" Rhea asked.

"I did not."

"So she's started spending her own money, then. Or has a loan in place?"

"Yes, unfortunately, she has a lot of money, and all of it was mine.

"What if she really wants to help, Marco?" asked Shannon.

"She's uncontrollable. She wants to be in charge, and she has no experience with building things."

Shannon spoke up again, objecting. "She told me in the interview she had a new project manager helping her run things."

"Yeah, I feel sorry for the guy," I added with a chuckle.

"What if her plan is a better one, Marco?" Rhea's partner asked.

"It's expensive getting a subdivision re-drawn. I can't imagine anything we missed. That's about thirty thousand dollars right down the drain. But you're right, we need to see what she's got up her sleeve."

"I'll go see what's been turned in, and then I'll look her up from the City file. I can send the redraw to Boston, if there is one?" Rhea asked.

"If you can get a set of plans, that would be awesome," I answered. As an afterthought, I added, "You guys get in there and dig around. I think you'll make the best spies. If it works out, I might be able to use you somewhere else."

"Where?" they both said in unison.

"Either of you ever been to Africa?"

WE DROVE BACK to Shannon's place, where I dropped her off. Before she went inside, she stopped and asked, "While you're gone, can I have a set of your old plans to look over, just for giggles?"

"Sure, I can get a set sent to you."

"Would you mind if I hang around the office in my spare time? I'm good with the phones, and a lot of people know who I am."

"I can't see that it would hurt. Let's talk about it tonight at dinner. What time, and do you need anything?"

"Just you. I even have more wine than I know what to do with. See you about five-thirty or six?"

"Or before."

"I'd like that too. You can pick up something sinful and chocolaty for dessert, if you like."

I had some great fantasies about chocolate syrup and whipped cream but decided I'd leave that for another time. This was going to be our good-bye dinner for now. I was grateful I'd have a few hours to myself to make some calls and check out of the hotel. I might even need a nap!

I needed to think about where we were going as a couple. She was being very good about not bringing it up, but I could tell it was on her mind.

The sex was great. We had fun. I loved surprising her. But all that would not hold up forever, if there was no future.

It was kind of dangerous to be jumping head-first into a relationship again. I hadn't exactly been the poster boy of success in that arena. But I knew deep down that if I walked away from this one, maybe there wouldn't be another.

Emily had taught me that.

"You gotta grab what happiness you can and hold onto it with all your heart. No regrets, Marco. We jump in without hesitation. If you need to do your deployment, go do it this one time, and I'll be here for you. But after that, I get the white dress, the flowers, the party and the honeymoon, and you're gonna wear your dress blues. Because when you come back, your ass is mine."

Those were the last words she'd told me. I wore my dress uniform at her funeral for the first time. I'd wear it a lot during the years as I lost people. Funerals, always funerals. So many men and women who didn't come home.

I'm still here. Maybe so I could get it right this time.

CHAPTER 18

Shannon

JUDIE POPPED IN unexpectedly. Looking over the mess in the kitchen, she knew something big was happening.

"*Fresh* pasta? Boy, I must have missed a whole lifetime. What in the world have you been up to?"

"It's too much to explain."

"Try me."

I pulled my hair off my forehead with the back of my hand. I could feel the flour trickling into my scalp, which meant now I had to make time for a shower and shampoo. I nearly burst into tears, which really surprised me. But the change between where I'd been when Judie and I last talked and where I was floating around now was so dramatic, it was just a bridge too far.

"Uh-oh, Shannon. Now you've got me worried," she gasped. "Your lower lip is protruding. What have you done?"

I didn't try holding back the tears. I placed my hands on the floured countertop and looked directly into her eyes. "I've gone and fallen in love with Marco Gambini."

"No! Say it isn't so!"

"I'm afraid it's true."

Judie gave me a puzzled look. "But, most people, when they fall in love, they're like dancing around the room, hugging babies and old men. They're whistling in the grocery store. Life is suddenly beautiful." She carefully delivered her kill shot. "You don't look that way."

"It's complicated."

"How could it be complicated? He's gorgeous. He's got a ton of money." She frowned and tilted her head slightly. "Unless…he's not in love with you. Tell me that isn't so."

"We haven't talked about it. But I think so."

"Ouch! Boy, he'd be off my list."

"He's worth it."

"Ew. I don't like the sounds of that. Shannon, it's not that complicated. Of course, I'm the one who never takes her own advice and has sex before there's a commitment. Like the Love Vixen lady says, get a ring and date first."

"I don't think she's ever fallen in love with her older sister's fiancé, who was a billionaire, and is now struggling to survive. He's got a lot on his plate."

"So you won't be the focus of his world, then. I'll bet right now all he wants to do is screw, am I right? He probably doesn't go calling his board meetings and signing contracts when you guys are working on the birds and the bees, fulfilling yourselves to your highest climax."

I felt a little guilty. She was right, or at least from what she knew she was right. I'd had more sex in the last three days than I'd had in three years.

I checked my timing. I needed to clean up the mess and start making the seafood alfredo topping for the fresh pasta, and mix the green salad. And I needed a shower.

I began wiping down the countertops.

"Oh, Shannon, here. Let me do that. You get yourself into the shower."

"No, I have to make the sauce!"

"Okay, but let me do the clean up here. You take that side of the kitchen while I clean up this one."

"You got it."

I was ruminating about all her questions. I hadn't even gotten to the part where I was going to accompany him to a real sultan's palace in five days. That I was taking a whole ten days off work, and I had to promise I'd do all kinds of things to get that favor, too. I hadn't told her I'd gotten drunk with his ex, either.

The tears were threatening to spill over my lower lids again as I added the butter and flour into one pan while sauteing the salmon and fresh scallops in another. I added some coriander and then some cheese until it melted into the butter mixture, then added the cream and stirred.

Judie put her arms around me. "What a problem to have, right?"

I chuckled, adding the fish mixture to the pan. I handed her the wooden spoon to stir since she'd cleaned up everything. I began rinsing vegetables for the green salad.

We worked in silence for about five minutes. Her mixture had begun to thicken, and I was done with the salad fixings, placing them in the refrigerator to chill.

I poured two huge glasses of red wine and handed her one. "We need to talk."

"You want to go out to the beach?"

"Not today, Judie. Maybe you can help me figure out something."

We sat in the living room, across from each other.

"Shoot," she said.

"I'm going with him to an island in the Indian Ocean, some sultan's pink palace. Supposed to be a really beautiful place. We're flying by private jet and then helicopter. This sultan has like thirteen wives, maybe more, he doesn't know. I'm to meet him in Boston in five days and we leave from there." I gulped down the whole glass of wine and gasped. Judie watched me with eyes as big as saucers. "And he still doesn't know who I am."

There. I'd told her everything.

She had barely touched her wine, which wasn't like her. Her gaze was focused on something on the floor because she was thinking about something. I diverted my focus to the side before she could make eye contact.

She took a sip and whispered, "I can't fix this."

I BARELY HAD my clothes on when Marco was at the front door, bringing me some of the roses from his room. He had something in a bright pink box tied with candy-striped string. I could smell it was going to taste divine.

"Here, take these, and I'll get my things from the car."

I added the roses to another vase, placing them at the table, and moved the spring bouquet onto the countertop. He entered with his leather bag, leaving it by the door instead of putting it in the bedroom. I began to get nervous.

He came to me, and I melted into his arms, feeling safe and loved. I inhaled the heady scent I never wanted to be without, and steeled my heart for whatever was to come next. His fingers laced through my hair.

"You want some wine?" I asked.

"Sure."

He was watching me carefully as I poured from another bottle. I was a little tipsy. Maybe that's what he was noticing.

He toasted my glass and remarked how good it was. I already knew that. I wanted to hear what was on his mind because his mood had changed.

"You want to eat?" I asked. "It's all ready."

"Smells wonderful. I'm starved." But neither of us moved.

If I wasn't careful, I'd be bursting out in tears, and nothing had really happened. I was just so sad all of a sudden. I had no basis for coming to that conclusion, but I felt like I'd blown the opportunity of a lifetime.

"Let's sit down," he said.

My knees stiffened. My stomach began to clench. It wouldn't be cool if I threw up in front of him, but I was headed there. I left my wine glass on the counter and took a seat across from him, just where I was when I talked to Judie this afternoon. I liked looking at Marco better.

"I have to tell you something, Shannon."

Oh, here it comes.

"I think I've taken advantage of you, and I'm so sorry I did that."

"I don't feel that way."

"But I do, and that's important to me. I just burst into your life, upsetting everything. I asked a lot from you."

"Nothing I wasn't willing to do. I'm a grownup. I didn't feel put upon. I've enjoyed being with you."

"But like you said, this world of mine? It isn't your world, and I wasn't being sensitive to that."

"It's a lot to get used to, don't you think?"

"I totally agree. And that's not my point."

"Okay." My heartbeat was still racing from the dark wolf in the forest.

"Remember when I talked about the woman I'd been in love with all those years ago? My first love?"

My veins turned to ice water. This was becoming a horror film. They found Emily, dug her up, and she was now a vampire She'd bit him and taken him back. Something like that.

"Her name was Emily. She was a lot like you. And it's got me thinking…"

He's figured it out! OMG he thinks I've lied to him!

"Marco, I know what you're going to say. I'm so very sorry. I shouldn't have done it. Can you forgive me?"

He suddenly looked confused. "Nonsense. You haven't done anything."

"I should have told you sooner is what I meant."

"But Shannon, we never spoke about it before today."

"I know, Marco. And that is all my fault."

"That's impossible. You could never do anything I

wouldn't love. That's what I'm trying to tell you. I'm in love with you, Shannon."

I couldn't speak. He slowly stood, came over to the couch, and knelt down in front of me, holding out a huge diamond ring. "I think I knew the first time I saw you. Everything fit into place so perfectly. Like we were long-lost friends, soulmates from another time and place."

"But…"

"Shannon, marry me. I waited too long before. She didn't want to wait. This doesn't have anything to do with her, but she taught me something. And I felt her come to me this afternoon, and it was like she was telling me I should stop waiting to join her, that I should find someone just like her, and do what I should have done before."

"But…"

"Don't you see? I never believe in these kinds of things. But it was like we were predestined for each other. You're the girl I've been looking for, waiting for my whole life."

I was in shock. I let him lift my left hand and slide the beautiful ring on my fourth finger. It was so heavy I felt like I'd fallen into the ocean, and that ring pulled me right down to the bottom of the sea, where I'd be forever.

CHAPTER 19

Marco

SHANNON DIDN'T REACT how I expected. I knew she didn't suspect that I would impulsively propose, but I didn't plan on her shivering, distance, and the look of pain on her face.

"What is this, Shannon? What's happened?"

"Nothing *happened*, but it's—"

I got to my feet, then sat next to her, my arm around her shoulder. She'd been playing with the ring, which was a little too loose. She was twisting it around and around her finger, staring down at her lap, gently rocking back and forth.

"I'm sorry about the size. I guessed. It will be easy to adjust." Was that the real problem going on with her?

She stopped rocking.

"Are you ill?" I persisted.

She carefully shook her head from side to side, her

eyes still focused downward.

I decided to just wait for her to tell me. Maybe she couldn't get the days off she hoped she could and was somehow upset about that. Maybe Rebecca paid her a visit. But something was definitely different, and I was worried, getting more so by the minute.

Then she turned toward me, our knees touching. She wrapped her arms around my neck brushed her cheek against mine. I felt her whole body shaking. When we parted, I could see she'd been crying.

Had I missed something? If she was averse to getting married, I'd try not to pressure her, but this wasn't the Shannon I had gotten to know. At last, she wiped her tears off her cheeks, removed the ring, and placed it in my palm, curling her fingers over mine and began to sob.

Through her tears, she said, "I can't accept this until you know the truth, Marco. I've been lying to you, and I feel horrible. I'm not the woman you think I am."

"I don't understand. What big dark secret do you have? I swear to you it won't matter."

"You don't know that," she mumbled, again wiping the tears from her cheeks. "I've been so dishonest with you."

Anger was beginning to boil in my belly. I'd been certain she would be thrilled at the prospect of spending the rest of her life with me. I felt punched in the gut. I was beginning to wonder if I knew anything about women because obviously something had happened and she was locking me out. I wanted answers and I wanted them fast.

I got up, shoved the ring in my pants pocket and started to pace. "This is complete bullshit, Shannon. I expect the truth from you. You better tell me the score or I'm walking right out of here and I'm not ever coming back."

Even that didn't make her spring to action. I felt a twinge of regret that I'd spoken to her harshly. Whatever it was, it was serious. I'd never seen her this way before.

I started guessing. "You're married."

She shook her head.

"You have five kids."

"God no."

"You have an incurable disease?"

"No, not that either."

"Does this have to do with Rebecca?"

"No." She inhaled deeply and then stared into my eyes. "The reason you thought everything was so familiar between us was that we *have* met before. We met over fifteen years ago."

She was waiting, searching my face to see if that helped me figure it out, but I still didn't have a clue.

"How did we meet? Fifteen years ago, you were

what? Ten?" I asked.

"Emily was my older sister. I'm Melanie Shannon Mabry. When I moved to Florida and began at TMBC, I picked a stage name. I used my middle name, Shannon. But—"

"Em always called you Shan," I said from memory, pictures of those days flooding my mind. The horrible pain and loss came back, and I felt like a terrible trick had been played on me by God.

"Marco, I was a preteen. Braces, bushy eyebrows, and skinny. I wore glasses in those days, and they were thick and huge. I got Lasix. I grew up, and when I shed all those things, I was a different person. Like a butterfly breaking out of its cocoon."

"So, you planned all this?" I demanded. I couldn't help but tighten my fingers into fists, trying to destress, but it wasn't helping.

"I didn't plan for all this, no. But I came to Boston to see you, to meet you, because I'd dreamed about you all those years. I just wanted to see—"

She began to tear up again.

"I never had what Em had, Marco. I wanted to see what that would feel like. I didn't intend to come insert myself into your life. I just wanted a taste, maybe just to experience something *she* had, maybe in some small way to bring her back. And that's stupid, I know."

I ground my teeth. I really thought I had experienced Emily talking to me, telling me to move on today. But it must have all been a figment of my imagination, because deep down inside, I must have sensed little Shan was just like her older sister. My mind had figured it out when my heart wasn't paying attention.

Here was yet again one more heartless betrayal. One other instance where I hadn't been paying attention. I was so intent on deepening this relationship out of pure fantasy, I was blindsided and I fell into the trap I'd fallen into before. Twice before.

The fact that she'd lied to me was so painful, I couldn't look at her any longer. I felt so completely ridiculous spending so much money on that diamond. Buying the red Bentley. What was I thinking? I didn't even know her. Heck, we never even talked. I hadn't asked her what it was like growing up. I didn't have a clue what I almost had gotten myself into.

"I do appreciate one thing, Shannon. I'm glad you told me now, not when we were halfway around the world, and thank God you told me before I entered into some sham marriage based on lies. It takes guts to tell the truth."

"No, I wasn't that noble. I thought you'd caught me. I knew I'd tell you eventually, but things got so hot and heavy, and then I never wanted it to end. I kept pushing it off into the distance, looking for a way, a time to tell you. But yes, that ring forced the truth out of me."

"So you basically *stalked* me?" I couldn't believe how vulnerable I was. "Am I that dumb?"

"No, it was chemistry. All that was real. I just came on stage under false pretenses. Don't beat yourself up, Marco. And because I used to watch the two of you, and when she was home on weekends from college, she used to tell me about you. I used to think about what it would feel like to kiss you. I didn't mean to take what was not mine."

I suddenly was transported back to that time. I leaned over, scrambled her hair on the top of her head, and said what I used to say all the time, "It's okay, kid. Things will turn out."

She broke down, hugging her knees. When she looked up at me at last, I saw those strong, unflinching eyes that I could get lost in. "I am so sorry. So very sorry. I never meant to hurt you. I know you'll never forgive me, but I want you to know, because I probably won't ever get the chance to say it again—I do love you, Marco. That part was real."

THE UNIVERSE HAD tilted, and I was in free fall. This was going to force me to re-think and re-evaluate every decision I'd recently made. My businesses were falling apart, and Rebecca hadn't done that. I did it. I was the one responsible for causing all this. I'd lost my focus, and now it suddenly had gotten worse.

Ten years ago I would have completely lost it with Shannon. But now, I was just numb. I could even understand why she did it, and that really surprised me. What I had the most difficulty with was that I didn't catch on. I pieced together the clues, and instead of coming up with a pink flamingo, I'd created a pelican. It was close. She was right. The chemistry was indeed there. But I was ill from knowing my firewall had been breached and my judgment was flawed. I acted with my heart instead of my head.

I vowed never to do that again.

I said good-bye and thanked her for our time together. I told her I needed to get somewhere all by myself and get my head on straight. I promised I'd let her know when I got back from D.C., and maybe we could talk. She told me she wanted to help out with the Trident Towers, asked my permission to see if she could get Rebecca to cooperate. She silently accepted my leaving without further drama, which I was grateful for.

I walked away knowing that she was wrong. She wasn't anything like Emily. If anything, Emily was the younger sister. Shannon was a complicated, confident woman who was even stronger than Rebecca, just in a softer way. She could move mountains with her smile.

She charmed me, and that was because I wanted to believe in love again. I *wanted* to be charmed.

It would be hard to watch her on the TV, thinking of all the things we'd done. I tried to fill in the blanks, because we never talked about it. How she grew up. How her poor parents were. They'd been so devastated with Em's passing. I didn't have any of that information. And maybe it was better that way.

I asked the Oceanis to store my convertible and to wash it every day, even park it out front if they wanted. I wasn't sure what I was going to do with the car.

I arranged for my pilot to come over early, and within three hours of my botched proposal of marriage, I was wheels up and headed back to Boston.

My pilot didn't ask too many questions and focused on his job, of course. He hadn't bothered hiring an attendant. I nestled down in the wool blankets and fluffy pillows and slept all the way until we landed. I vowed I'd stop being so indulgent with the alcohol, the desserts, the exquisite foods, and go back to my "Go-To" diet, and I'd start working out again. I had to get through these next few days. If I could get my body into action, focus on re-connecting with all the D.C. allies I lost touch with as I fought off the attorneys, and when I got back out into the field, covered in dust and jumping from airplanes again, I would start to heal. Hiding, rescuing, defending people and leading escape missions would bring me back to life. That's the only item on my agenda, while I cleaned up the pieces of my broken fortune.

Alone.

Maybe Em had taken that happy family and the true love portion of my life to the grave with her. It was only now, fifteen years later, that I finally caught on.

But at least I caught on.

Shannon would land on her feet, because that's what she deserved. It wouldn't be useful to be bitter about it. That never was her intention. We both got caught up in that fantasy and were equally at fault. I didn't want to expend the energy blaming her, because it wasn't true.

As my driver pulled up to the Bachelor Towers, I handled my own bags, stopped by to pick up a Midnight in Manhattan from Ollie and went right to my floor without answering any questions.

The sterile place felt like a shiny gilded cage as I walked in all alone once more. I had to get more paintings on the wall, some color in there.

I removed my tie, brought my drink into the bedroom, exhausted, and began to get ready for bed early. The sun was still up.

In the shower, I thought about Shannon. As I tucked myself into the sheets naked, I thought about Shannon.

Yeah, I had been bitten by the snake of love, just like the sultan had advised. A tiny regret tugged at my heart. It was unfair, but it was definitely there. I'd looked forward to bringing her back here, remembering our beautiful first night together. I wanted her in every part of my life. How in the world would I ever forget how I felt with her? Even as determined as I was, there would always be that hole, that place where I felt safe in her love.

I thought about all the lovely things we would have done in this bed, in this apartment, had looked forward to.

If she were here.

I fell asleep with a smile on my face.

CHAPTER 20

Shannon

I'D NEVER CALLED in sick before, but I did today. I needed a day of sleep and walks on the beach. I needed to face the reality of what I'd done, look inside my heart, and try to figure out why it all went so wrong. Why did I think that not telling him would make things any easier later on? It was a stupid, foolish idea. It was important to get it settled in my own head first. Then I'd meet the world and embrace the rest of my life.

But I did prove one thing. I devised a plan, executed it, and went for broke. And I nearly made it. Never again would I use a lie, even a white lie, as a coverup for being real. My choice was real. It was how I did it that doomed the mission. I should have told him that day when he said, "No more secrets, Shannon." That would have been the perfect time.

So many of the wonderful qualities Marco had were

complementary to my own. We made a good pair. I resigned myself to the fact that if there was one man I could run off with in reckless abandon, there had to be another. I didn't need five or six. Just one more. When the right time came along. I completely pushed out of my mind the worry that perhaps there would never be another. That there was only one man for me. That I'd met him, fallen in love with him honestly and with my full heart, and that my methods were completely wrong. But I had to believe that, one day, there would come another.

On Tuesday, I went back to work and told Jared that I wasn't flying off to a pink palace in the Indian Ocean. He almost looked disappointed for me. If he studied my face any closer, he'd see my puffy eyes—the result from an all-day crying jag.

It had taken Marco several days before he called me again after our first encounter in Boston, but I didn't expect he'd really call me this time, even though he said he would. I braced for that. Accepted it as the consequence of my actions. I respected his boundaries now, unlike before. I wasn't going to delude myself or pick weeds in his garden, because it wasn't my garden.

But it sort of felt like making amends to show up as a volunteer at his center. It made me a better person, and I needed that. Nobody expected it, and I even asked permission, just to keep it clean. I intended on doing this in and around my work schedule, since I had no social life now.

I didn't expect any resumption of our former relationship, so I concentrated on doing more meditation and stretching. I started eating less and drinking more water. I knew in time it would stop hurting so much. Time and the beach.

The beach heals everything. It was my favorite plaque on my wall. I would live by that motto every day until I was whole again.

I even accepted Jared's invitation to have a drink later in the week. I thought he was going to fall off his chair when I said yes.

I stopped by the project after work on Wednesday and helped Dax's group make calls to donors from our curated list. I used my real name, since anonymity was what I was going for. I was just doing the pure work and not getting celebrity status out of it. It was the least I could do after creating such an upset.

Judie and I planned to go to the movies on the weekend. We both had a lot to catch up on together. She loved hearing about Marco and how he lived his life in the old days before either of us knew very much about him. We made up stories about what we'd do if we inherited hundreds of millions of dollars. And now I realized how shallow that had been. It was Marco I had fallen in love with, not his lifestyle, his handsome body, or his warrior mentality. I loved the part of him that reached out to me and trusted me, before I shattered it. I would try to think of him that way. Always.

Rhea got a set of plans from the County, and before she sent them to Marco, I looked them over. Rebecca had submitted extensive changes, she pointed out.

"The cost of concrete for these foundations will be at least double what it was before."

"How so?""

"Well see, she's used the full forty-two-foot height, adding additional units for a third floor, complete with balconies. Many of the exterior windows had been changed to sliding glass doors for access to those outdoor places. That also means there will be new engineering costs and calculations. We don't have earthquakes, but we have tropical storms and hurricanes to consider. More stories, more windows. More balconies, more weight."

I could see, as she pointed out all the details, Rhea understood that this project wasn't anything like the original proposed plan.

"She's going to have to go before the design review, but maybe the planning commission too," sighed Rhea. "I wonder if she knew that."

"So that would delay the project, then."

"Yes, I think we're looking at maybe six months, a year additional, maybe longer."

"I don't get it. Why do you think she's doing this?"

"Well, it is a much nicer design. I mean it's really pretty, but it's going to require a lot more money. I hope she's got unlimited funds."

I wondered if she'd gotten a wealthy backer.

"Did you try to get hired on?"

"That was a no-go. She recognized me right away. Dax too. And she has some guy who used to work for Marco there too. I've met him a time or two."

"Who was that?"

"He's an accountant, I think. Calls him her project manager."

I decided I should speak to Rebecca, see if she would open up about her plans. Maybe I could still be useful for Marco.

Judie was against it when I told her later on.

"That's not a good sign, Shannon. You need space. You need to distance yourself from all this. Time to move on. Didn't you get the memo?"

"I am moving on. This is how I move on. By doing something important for someone I care about."

"No you're not." She sighed, getting ready to give me the lecture I probably deserved. "This is what got you into trouble before. Face the facts. Move on so you can make the clean break. It will continue to cause pain if you even have the possibility of running into him again."

"I don't think that will bother me."

"Would you listen to yourself? You must be joking, Shannon. You're setting yourself up for a huge fall. What happens when he brings his new love into the office, or you see his picture in the society column on the arm of a beautiful heiress or something? You'll be looking for him everywhere."

"Am I that obsessed, still?"

"Yes! Finally something smart out of your mouth. It's unhealthy to hang on."

"Okay, then. I'll speak to Rebecca, communicate to Rhea what I've learned, if anything, and then move on."

"Unbelievable. You are the most stubborn woman I know, and I know a lot of stubborn women too! That's what you said when you went to Boston—'just to get a glimpse, have a drink with him.' That's what got you into trouble in the first place. Now do you get it?"

"Thanks for your advice."

"Which you're not going to take."

"I can't. I want to do something good for him, and then I'll exit the stage and go home."

I left her shaking her head, mumbling things loud enough for me to hear as I walked to my car.

I didn't pay any attention.

REBECCA'S SYRUPY SWEET demeanor was as overpowering as her perfume. She was packing, returning back to New York, but agreed to meet with me.

"All my friends loved the interview, Shannon. I should hire you as my press secretary. Want a job?"

Of all the things she could offer me, that one made me laugh.

"What's so funny?"

I knew I couldn't be honest with her. And here I went again, making things up. I probably should look into becoming a private investigator, the way I snuck around, spying under false pretenses.

I decided to keep it as clean as I could. "Nothing. Just hit me oddly, for some reason."

"You have quite an interest in our project here. Would you consider working on it?"

She was actually serious! That gave me the segue to ask some of the questions I needed answered.

"Let me ask you this first, if you don't mind."

"Go right ahead." She placed a cosmetic bag, bulging with tubes of creams and makeup, on top of her folded clothes, with a towel separating it. She saw me eyeing the towel. "Yes, I steal towels all the time, if they're good ones."

"I—I wasn't going there. I just noticed it. That's all. No judgment."

She continued packing but was nearly done, so I had to think of something quick.

"Can I buy you lunch? Or do you have a plane to catch?"

She checked her watch. "I have forty minutes before the car comes to take me to the airport. If we can order and finish in forty minutes, I'm all yours."

Rebecca made a big point of telling the waitress we were in a hurry and ordered her lunch without using the menu. I just agreed to the same thing to make things easier.

"What do you want to know? And you're not recording this, right?"

"No, ma'am." I thanked the waitress for our waters. "How did you meet Marco?"

She sat up straighter, her eyebrows rising under her bangs. "At a party in Coronado. A buddy of his was getting married. I knew the bride. The groom was a SEAL. We danced. We drank too much, and the rest is history."

"No big romantic date, then? The stars didn't fall from the sky the night you met?"

"He was in a mood. He'd just lost someone. He wanted to forget." Her eyes sparkled with deep dark undertones. "I liked the way he screwed. I was hooked." She followed it up with a pert smile.

I knew the feeling well.

"But in time, you fell in love, right?"

"I think he did. We got busy. He was all fire, going

out to play on those ridiculous missions of his. I loved that he was so happy to see me. I enjoyed it when he was gone. I loved it when he came back." She smiled again, like she was withholding a secret. "I became indispensable. He has a real blind spot for people he tells himself he cares about."

"*Tells* himself? I'm sure you loved each other."

"Oh, I never loved him. I loved being around him. I don't think I'm capable of love."

I must have looked shocked because she continued.

"The only thing he truly loves is his job, his missions, his brothers. They are an old school of guys who leave a trail of ex-wives and kids behind them. They usually don't manage their money well. Marco was the exception to that. But still, when it came down to it, he'd rather go do something dangerous, make money for others, than enjoy being a husband, a father."

"Is that why you never had kids?"

"I couldn't have any. I don't think he's the fatherly type."

"I'm so sorry."

"Don't be. I was raped when I was sixteen, had a complication of a pregnancy I never should have had, and just like that, no babies for me. One of my father's friends. He should have been charged and sent to prison for what he did to me. I decided that day that I wasn't going to let any man do that to me again. I made what I could out of it. Hated my father for the rest of my life. It actually became a blessing in disguise because I could do things other girls couldn't. I expressed myself through sex. It opened up a whole new world for me, so I grabbed it and ran. I don't spend any time on regrets. What about you?"

"It has to mean something for me. I am very guilty of wanting to be alone a lot. My books are my best friends, my boyfriends too."

"You'll have to meet my new manager, Frank. He used to work for Marco. He's married, but he's not a bad lay."

I was repulsed.

"Oh! I didn't steal him away from Marco," she said, holding up her hand, "if that's what you're thinking. I do have some scruples."

Except you made him cheat on his wife.

"He's not permanent. I'm still looking. And who knows? This project takes a year or two longer to complete? You never know. Marco might get lonely and come walking back through my door. I'll take him with welcome arms. We were a great team. I miss all those sweaty nights."

I suddenly saw what she was doing. She was never going to let go of him. He had way underestimated her. His only option was to quit the project, and be done with her.

But I knew he couldn't do that.

I asked her a few more questions, and we agreed to talk again after she got settled in New York. I told her I'd do a follow-up piece for TMBC later, and she was delighted.

"Think about what I offered you. I could teach you a lot, Shannon."

If she only knew what a sneak and a cheat I had been as well, I think she would have been impressed. But I didn't want any more of that. The bitter taste in my mouth was hard to get rid of.

I missed the fresh kisses and whispers. I missed the soft, trusting intimacy we had. I wanted what was real. My heart told me my love for him was real, but I knew I had to carefully bury it. I still loved Emily, too, and always would. Loving her wasn't predicated on me being around her every day or even visiting her grave.

Just like it would be okay to love Marco still, and never see him again.

CHAPTER 21

Marco

My meetings in D.C. went well. I got a track on a couple of projects the State Department was orchestrating, selling protective gear for IEDs in several third-world countries. I would be the middleman, and because it wasn't arms, it came under our foreign aid categories and didn't need congressional approval.

My company in Vietnam made these blue "ponchos." They could stop anything but a .50 caliber round and were very effective for roadside bombs.

We were also selling these to other contractors, and I was given the lead to a large award I didn't get because I was indisposed. But I could sell them the goods, and that was almost as valuable. I knew there were some Chinese firms who were trying to duplicate my product. I was scrambling to move my factory to the Midwest so I could say it was one hundred percent American made. And I had to be realistic, my designs and fabric would be copied. It was only a matter of time.

I interviewed a couple of candidates for the CFO position, two in person and one via video conference. Bob had done a great job working with the HR Department, finding candidates. He was also pleased to learn I was headed to India.

"Rebecca's attorney has quit. He called me yesterday to tell me he thought things would be quieter."

"He can say that?"

"Professional courtesy. He's resigning his firm, going into the Peace Corps, if you can believe such a thing. I think he's lost his taste for blood."

"That's what she does. Uses people and spits them out," I added.

Bob was watching me.

"You look tired, Marco. I think the trip will do you good. The sultan really stepped up to the plate this time for you. You're the luckiest guy I know."

"Spoken by a man who only feels comfortable in three-piece suits."

"Okay, I didn't like that, but it was justified. But I'm bringing this up because you've been driving so hard and fighting so long. Time to come home from deployment. At some point in your life, you have to learn to enjoy it."

"I do enjoy it. I enjoy the hunt. Exceeding capacity.

Winning in court occasionally is actually fun, now. Except for the cost."

"I'm not reducing my fees."

"Wasn't asking."

"You're forty-five?"

"Watch it. Forty-three."

"Time to start raising a family, or raising someone else's family. You know lots of good men who never came back. Their wives are good women, Marco. Doing the best they can. Go pick one, get married, and fulfill someone else's dreams who you respect. Raise the kids to love their father. And learn to be one. I'm going to personally go out on a limb and say all these things, because after all the wars are over, you know what we have?"

"Not sure what you're saying."

"We have a country to come home to. Some people don't have that."

"Tell me about it. I'm headed to one soon."

"I can't even imagine what that will be like, taking care of those boys who have been raised in a pink palace. Kids who spend more money on their shoes than some of those people they will be working with earn their whole lifetime. Do you think what they're doing will make a difference?"

"Oh, hell yes. They need housing."

"If they can keep it privately held. Until some new

warlord comes into power and takes everything away or blows it up."

"You've been reading too much, Bob," I said as I stood and shook his hand. "And in answer to your question, it's just like the graffiti problem."

He angled his head and furrowed his brow. "I don't understand."

"The secret to getting rid of it is to keep painting over it over and over again. They put it up. You take it down. You know when you're taking it down that they'll tag it again, but you keep doing it. Someday, they grow up, or move, or go elsewhere, and it starts to change. Some day. We got to keep thinking about someday. The sultan will build these houses, and yes, some of them will get destroyed. But someday, someone else will build houses, and then maybe another, and eventually, they will be allowed to stand. There will be houses to pass down to their kids and grandkids. And the people won't live in fear anymore."

"God dammit, Marco. You're a fuckin' optimist."

That was funny. I laughed. I'd never thought that about myself. And then it hit me, I believed in the Happily Ever After, like those books Emily used to read. I knew that someday everything would turn out.

'It will be okay, kid.'

CHAPTER 22

Shannon

I WAS RUSHING to get to makeup in time for my first afternoon report. There was a big storm coming, and people would be tuning in to find out where it was going to land.

Sandy commented on how tanned I'd been. "You are spending a lotta time outdoors. It's good for you, Shannon. Your skin is lovely today."

"I've been watching what I'm eating and, yes, been taking more walks on the beach."

"I used to do that when I was younger, too. You get older, and you just don't do those things any longer."

"I plan never to stop."

I had started to feel better with each passing hour. Day by day, I found meaning in Marco's project. I enjoyed the crazy people at the station more, even that bastard Clarence Thompson. We, openly pretend-flirted on the air, since we both knew if he tried anything, he'd get fired, and at his age, he was probably unemployable. And I saw him with new eyes. I saw the vacant part of his life. The guy was lonely.

'I guess it takes one to know one.' My mother used to say that all the time. Emily used to tease me with that when I called her a rat or a cheater or when I tried to take the biggest piece of cake. Funny, I had forgotten how much we actually did fight over little things. In the wash that was necessary to heal my heart, what also was lost were those little details. I tended to think of her as perfect, of our childhood as perfect. But she could be a little shit, too. I took it as a good sign that a lot of things were healing inside me. My internal housekeeping was redecorating, freshening up the curtains, recovering couches, and painting the walls a different color.

I stepped onto the set, adjusted my microphone, and squinted at the teleprompter. I hoped that this didn't mean my eye surgery was failing. I blinked several times, and the letters got clearer and larger.

"Well, now we come to my favorite part of the day. We have Shannon Marr here to tell us what's coming up along the Gulf. You have any fun plans for this weekend?" Clarence asked, winking at me, daring me to say something racy.

"Just some good beach time, Clarence," I answered.

"Oh darn," he said as he clicked his fingers. With

his hand up to his mouth, as an aside to the audience, he whispered, "At my age, the only way I get my thrills is by listening to her talk about her boyfriends."

Someone had turned the canned laughter off. Clarence looked up above him, as if he'd been suddenly covered with bugs.

"Hey, I thought that was funny! Oh, well, give us the weather, Shannon."

"Thanks so much. Well..." And then I began moving my hands in front of the green screen, watching the monitor to make sure I didn't worry all our Tampa Bay people by misplacing the eye of the next storm smack on their town, instead of well out in the middle of the Gulf of Mexico. I did that once, and the newsroom was flooded with panicked calls.

"And that about wraps it up. Oh, and we have a special programming note I'm supposed to read."

The screen went white for a couple of seconds and then letters began appearing. I inhaled and began.

"Shannon, will you—" I stopped because it wasn't any special programming message. I heard laughing around the set. Out of the darkness, behind one of the camera operators, walked Marco, dressed in a stunning royal blue suit with a red tie, holding a bouquet of red roses. And he was smiling, headed right for me.

I looked around the stage. Even Clarence was grinning at his podium. Everyone must have been in on it, because they kept me live. Marco knelt before me, held out the beautiful diamond ring I'd seen all too briefly the other night, and asked, "Shannon Marr, I've been a complete fool. Will you forgive me, and will you agree to be my wife?"

They didn't even wait for my answer before the canned cheering and clapping was played. I looked into his face, the handsome face of my one true warrior, the love of my life, the man who was so right for me in too many ways to count.

And I said yes, even though everyone else was already celebrating.

Marco slipped the ring on my left hand fourth finger, and it fit perfectly. Of course it did.

I kissed him, as he stood and properly showed me, live, like a hurricane headed for the Gulf, that he loved me and would never leave me again.

I touched the sparkling jewel and whispered, "What does all this mean, Marco? What are we going to do with Rebecca?"

"I'm not marrying Rebecca again. Did that. Didn't work out so well. And for the record, I'm not asking you to either."

"I'm serious."

"So am I." He winked at me. "Waiting for Rebecca to start playing nice and not being a thorn in my side would be like waiting until there were no more wars overseas before we get married. I don't have that much time. Even you don't either."

"But doesn't it bother you?"

"It has nothing to do with my decision."

I don't want to quit my job. You live in Boston. How is this going to work?"

"Well, since I won't be a bachelor, I should probably move out of the Bachelor Towers. I thought maybe you'd be able to put me up at your place until I could get that house built."

"House?"

"The lot on the bluffs? I own it. I want to build a house there. For us."

"But what about my bungalow?"

It took him a couple of seconds. His eyes blinked fast while he thought of something to say. "You always manage to throw curve balls, don't you?"

"Well, I was just thinking—"

He turned to the camera man. "Is this all being recorded?"

"No, we're off the air."

"Could you turn off the lights, please?" he asked.

It was dark, with a deep blueish reflection on the equipment, the desks and the metal surfaces of the studio to keep people from tripping.

Marco cleared his throat. "Let me try this again. Shannon," he said, his patience being tested to the max.

"Would you like to live in your house or the new one I'll be building? It would be big enough for your parents to come visit. If we have children, they can each have their own bedroom. But, my dear, if you say no, then we'll live at your sweet little home. And I'll pay rent."

He said it with a completely straight face. With tears streaming down mine, I crushed the roses he was holding between us, hugged him, and whispered, "I'd like to do both. I don't want to sell the house I lived in when I met and fell in love with you. We can take vacations there, just down the street."

He smiled as we parted. "Anything you want, sweetheart."

I reached up to touch his face. "Then I want you to kiss me."

You are going to see more of Marco and Shannon next year, as they make tough decisions, battle the unstoppable Rebecca and find their way to that peaceful place at the Florida Gulf Coast to eventually settle down.

This was their first adventure together as a couple. But the adventure is just starting! Stay tuned for more books in the Bone Frog Bachelor Series, a spin-off and continuation of the saga.

Do you want more Florida white sugary sand beach? Read Book 5 in the Sunset SEALs series, **The House At Sunset**, coming out just in time for Thanksgiving, but you can preorder it now. It's the continuation of Aimee and Andy Carr as they work on their DIY project and uncover the mystery of a long-forgotten love story, while Aimee searches for her lost brother.

Experience the magic and glory of the sunsets and love stories at Sunset Beach.

So you don't miss a thing, be sure to sign up for Sharon's Newsletter or follow her on Goodreads, Amazon or BookBub.

ABOUT THE AUTHOR

NYT and USA Today best-selling author Sharon Hamilton's award-winning Navy SEAL Brotherhood series have been a fan favorite from the day the first one was released. They've earned her the coveted Amazon author ranking of #1 in Romantic Suspense, Military Romance and Contemporary Romance categories, as well as in Gothic Romance for her Vampires of Tuscany and Guardian Angels. Her characters follow a sometimes rocky road to redemption through passion and true love.

Now that he's out of the Navy, Sharon can share with her readers that her son spent a decade as a Navy SEAL, and he's the inspiration for her books.

Her Golden Vampires of Tuscany are not like any vamps you've read about before, since they don't go to ground and can walk around in the full light of the sun.

Her Guardian Angels struggle with the human charges they are sent to save, often escaping their vanilla world of Heaven for the brief human one. You won't find any of these beings in any Sunday school class.

She lives in Sonoma County, California with her

husband and her Doberman, Tucker. A lifelong organic gardener, when she's not writing, she's getting *verra verra* dirty in the mud, or wandering Farmers Markets looking for new Heirloom varieties of vegetables and flowers. She and her husband plan to cure their wanderlust (or make it worse) by traveling in their Diesel Class A Pusher, Romance Rider. Starting with this book, all her writing will be done on the road.

She loves hearing from her fans:
Sharonhamilton2001@gmail.com

Her website is:
sharonhamiltonauthor.com

Find out more about Sharon, her upcoming releases, appearances and news when you sign up for Sharon's newsletter.

Facebook:
facebook.com/SharonHamiltonAuthor

Twitter:
twitter.com/sharonlhamilton

Pinterest:
pinterest.com/AuthorSharonH

Amazon:
amazon.com/Sharon-Hamilton/e/B004FQQMAC

BookBub:
bookbub.com/authors/sharon-hamilton

Youtube:
youtube.com/channel/UCDInkxXFpXp_4Vnq08ZxMBQ

Soundcloud:
soundcloud.com/sharon-hamilton-1

Sharon Hamilton's Rockin' Romance Readers:
facebook.com/groups/sealteamromance

Sharon Hamilton's Goodreads Group:
goodreads.com/group/show/199125-sharon-hamilton-readers-group

Visit Sharon's Online Store:
sharon-hamilton-author.myshopify.com

Join Sharon's Review Teams:

eBook Reviews:
sharonhamiltonassistant@gmail.com

Audio Reviews:
sharonhamiltonassistant@gmail.com

***Life** is one fool thing after another.*

***Love** is two fool things after each other.*

REVIEWS

PRAISE FOR THE GOLDEN VAMPIRES OF TUSCANY SERIES

"Well to say the least I was thoroughly surprise. I have read many Vampire books, from Ann Rice to Kym Grosso and few other Authors, so yes I do like Vampires, not the super scary ones from the old days, but the new ones are far more interesting far more human than one can remember. I found Honeymoon Bite a totally engrossing book, I was not able to put it down, page after page I found delight, love, understanding, well that is until the bad bad Vamp started being really bad. But seeing someone love another person so much that they would do anything to protect them, well that had me going, then well there was more and for a while I thought it was the end of a beautiful love story that spanned not only time but, spanned Italy and California. Won't divulge how it ended, but I did shed a few tears after screaming but Sharon Hamilton did not let me down, she took me on amazing trip that I loved, look forward to reading another Vampire book of hers."

"An excellent paranormal romance that was exciting, romantic, entertaining and very satisfying to read. It had me anticipating what would happen next many times over, so much so I could not put it down and even finished it up in a day. The vampires in this book were different from your average vampire, but I enjoy different variations and changes to the same old stuff. It made for a more unpredictable read and more adventurous to explore! Vampire lovers, any paranormal readers and even those who love the romance genre will enjoy Honeymoon Bite."

"This is the first non-Seal book of this author's I have read and I loved it. There is a cast-like hierarchy in this vampire community with humans at the very bottom and Golden vampires at the top. Lionel is a dark vampire who are servants of the Goldens. Phoebe is a Golden who has not decided if she will remain human or accept the turning to become a vampire. Either way she and Lionel can never be together since it is forbidden.

I enjoyed this story and I am looking forward to the next installment."

"A hauntingly romantic read. Old love lost and new love found. Family, heart, intrigue and vampires. Grabbed my attention and couldn't put down. Would definitely recommend."

PRAISE FOR THE SEAL BROTHERHOOD SERIES

"Fans of Navy SEAL romance, I found a new author to feed your addiction. Finely written and loaded delicious with moments, Sharon Hamilton's storytelling satisfies like a thick bar of chocolate." —Marliss Melton, bestselling author of the *Team Twelve* Navy SEALs series

"Sharon Hamilton does an EXCELLENT job of fitting all the characters into a brotherhood of SEALS that may not be real but sure makes you feel that you have entered the circle and security of their world. The stories intertwine with each book before…and each book after and THAT is what makes Sharon Hamilton's SEAL Brotherhood Series so very interesting. You won't want to put down ANY of her books and they will keep you reading into the night when you should be sleeping. Start with this book…and you will not want to stop until you've read the whole series and then…you will be waiting for Sharon to write the next one." (5 Star Review)

"Kyle and Christy explode all over the pages in this first book, *[Accidental SEAL]*, in a whole new series of SEALs. If the twist and turns don't get your heart jumping, then maybe the suspense will. This is a must read for those that are looking for love and adventure with a little sloppy love thrown in for good measure." (5 Star Review)

PRAISE FOR THE
BAD BOYS OF SEAL TEAM 3 SERIES

"I love reading this series! Once you start these books, you can hardly put them down. The mix of romance and suspense keeps you turning the pages one right after another! Can't wait until the next book!" (5 Star Review)

"I love all of Sharon's Seal books, but *[SEAL's Code]* may just be her best to date. Danny and Luci's journey is filled with a wonderful insight into the Native American life. It is a love story that will fill you with warmth and contentment. You will enjoy Danny's journey to become a SEAL and his reasons for it. Good job Sharon!" (5 Star Review)

PRAISE FOR THE
BAND OF BACHELORS SERIES

"*[Lucas]* was the first book in the Band of Bachelors series and it was a phenomenal start. I loved how we got to see the other SEALs we all love and we got a look at Lucas and Marcy. They had an instant attraction, and their love was very intense. This book had it all, suspense, steamy romance, humor, everything you want in a riveting, outstanding read. I can't wait to read the next book in this series." (5 Star Review)

PRAISE FOR THE TRUE BLUE SEALS SERIES

"Keep the tissues box nearby as you read *True Blue SEALs: Zak* by Sharon Hamilton. I imagine more than I wish to that the circumstances surrounding Zak and Amy are all too real for returning military personnel and their families. Ms. Hamilton has put us right in the middle of struggles and successes that these two high school sweethearts endure. I have read several of Sharon Hamilton's military romances but will say this is the most emotionally intense of the ones that I have read. This is a well-written, realistic story with authentic characters that will have you rooting for them and proud of those who serve to keep us safe. This is an author who writes amazing stories that you love and cry with the characters. Fans of Jessica Scott and Marliss Melton will want to add Sharon Hamilton to their list of realistic military romance writers." (5 Star Review)

"Dear FATHER IN HEAVEN,

If I may respectfully say so sometimes you are a strange God. Though you love all mankind,

It seems you have special predilections too.

You seem to love those men who can stand up alone who face impossible odds, Who challenge every bully and every tyrant ~

Those men who know the heat and loneliness of Calvary. Possibly you cherish men of this stamp because you recognize the mark of your only son in them.

Since this unique group of men known as the SEALs know Calvary and suffering, teach them now the mystery of the resurrection ~ that they are indestructible, that they will live forever because of their deep faith in you.

And when they do come to heaven, may I respectfully warn you, Dear Father, they also know how to celebrate. So please be ready for them when they insert under your pearly gates.

Bless them, their devoted Families and their Country on this glorious occasion.

We ask this through the merits of your Son, Christ Jesus the Lord, Amen."

By Reverend E.J. McMalhon S.J. LCDR, CHC, USN
Awards Ceremony SEAL Team One
1975 At NAB, Coronado